LESSONS FROM THE HEART

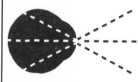

This Large Print Book carries the
Seal of Approval of N.A.V.H.

LESSONS FROM THE HEART

DOROTHY CLARK

THORNDIKE PRESS

An imprint of Thomson Gale, a part of The Thomson Corporation

Detroit • New York • San Francisco • New Haven, Conn. • Waterville, Maine • London

Copyright © 2006 by Dorothy Clark.

Thorndike Press, an imprint of The Gale Group.

Thomson and Star Logo and Thorndike are trademarks and Gale is a registered trademark used herein under license.

Thorndike Press® Large Print Christian Romance.

The text of this Large Print edition is unabridged.

Other aspects of the book may vary from the original edition.

Set in 16 pt. Plantin.

LIBRARY OF CONGRESS CATALOGING-IN-PUBLICATION DATA

Clark, Dorothy.
    Lessons from the heart / by Dorothy Clark.
        p. cm. — (Thorndike Press large print Christian romance)
    ISBN-13: 978-1-4104-0391-9 (hardcover : alk. paper)
    ISBN-10: 1-4104-0391-2 (hardcover : alk. paper)
    1. Large type books. I. Title.
PS3603.L359L47 2008
813'.6—dc22   2007037681

Published in 2008 by arrangement with Harlequin Books S.A.

Printed in the United States of America on permanent paper
10 9 8 7 6 5 4 3 2 1

Be ye not unequally yoked together with unbelievers: for what fellowship hath righteousness with unrighteousness and what communion hath light with darkness?

— 2 Corinthians 6:14

Can two walk together, unless they be agreed?

— Amos 3:3

This book is dedicated, with affection and deep appreciation, to my editor, Krista Stroever, who gently and kindly eases me over the rough patches of the writing process with her humor, patience, enthusiasm and wonderful editing talent. And to my agent and friend, Joyce Hart. Without her faith in my writing, this book would not exist.

Thank you to the ladies of the Literacy Volunteers of Cattaraugus County for graciously answering my questions about this important work. And to all of the volunteers at all of the literacy centers across America for their dedication in helping others to a better life.

And I must extend my special thanks to Elizabeth Curtis, a sister ACFW member, who *immediately* stepped forward to answer my cry for help with the medical information I needed for this book. It must be all that E.R. trauma nurse training that makes her so quick to react! Whatever it is, she saved my skin. I couldn't have written this book without your expert advice, Elizabeth. So again, thank you.

"Commit thy works unto the Lord, and thy thoughts shall be established."

Your word is truth. Thank You, Jesus. To You be the glory.

CHAPTER ONE

David Carlson glanced at his mirrors, signaled then pulled over into the turn lane. Disappointment rode his shoulders. He needed a big story. He was so close to gaining a position among the top echelon of reporters at *The Herald,* and now the rumor about graft in the city's transportation department he'd been investigating had fizzled into nothing but a disgruntled employee trying to get his boss in trouble.

David frowned and made the right turn onto Monroe Street. He was feeling a little disgruntled himself. One thing was sure, he wouldn't find his big story this afternoon. At least not until he cleared away this minor one. He scanned the buildings on the right, looking for numbers — 1422 . . . 1424 . . . Ah! There it was.

David flipped on his blinker, pulled into the parking lot of the Westwood Literacy Center then glanced at his watch. Five minutes early. Perfect. *Okay, Professor Stiles, let's get this over with!*

Erin Kelly hurried down the hallway, crossed the entrance and stuck her head around the open office door. "You wanted to see me, Professor?"

"Yes, yes. Come in, Erin, I'll just be a minute." The elderly man rummaged through a towering stack of papers on his desk, scowled then ran his hand through his thinning gray hair. "I had it here yesterday. . . ."

He thumbed his way through another pile. "I don't know why I can never find —"

Erin hooted. He scowled up at her. "Are you laughing at me, young lady?"

"Not at all." She gave him a cheeky grin. "I'm laughing at your expectations."

"Humph!"

The snort was one of fond affection. Erin's grin widened. She gestured toward the litter of books, magazines and miscellaneous folders and papers that covered the large desk. "Do you really expect to find a specific item in that mess?"

"I do."

She took a brave step forward. "Then perhaps if you tell me what you're searching for, I could help."

10

"I don't *need* any help! That's what's wrong." The professor directed a baleful look toward his secretary in the entrance room and raised his voice. "That *woman* was in here straightening up again. She can't leave anything alone."

"I only threw away things that were *growing*."

The words floated in over Erin's shoulder. She laughed and turned toward the door. "Good one, Alice!"

The secretary grinned at her, then faced the other way as the outer door opened.

Erin shifted her gaze. A tall, broad-shouldered, *gorgeous* man entered. He looked vaguely familiar. She searched through the files of memories in her head as she watched him walk over to Alice.

"Good afternoon. I'm David Carlson. I have an appointment with Professor Robert Stiles."

The sound of his voice did it. Recognition dawned. David Carlson appeared occasionally on *Channel Four News.* What was he — ?

"Hah! I've got it! One o'clock!"

Erin turned back to find the professor waving a scrap of paper through the air like a flag of triumph.

"That's what I thought, just couldn't

11

remember for sure." The professor ducked his head and squinted at her over the top of his glasses. "Some newshound called the other day. He wants to interview me about —"

Someone cleared their throat behind her. The professor stopped speaking and shifted his gaze to a point above and beyond her head. His gray eyebrows drew together. "Who are you?"

"The newshound."

There was a trace of amusement in the deep voice. Erin stole a sidelong glance as David Carlson stepped up beside her and extended his hand over the desk.

"I hope I'm not interrupting anything important. Your secretary told me to come in. I'm David Carlson of *The Herald,* Professor Stiles. It's good to make your acquaintance."

"Humph. Too early to know that." Her boss waved an age-spotted hand in her direction. "This is my program coordinator, Erin Kelly."

David Carlson swung his handsome, impeccably groomed head her way. She looked up into his intelligent, alert, gray-blue eyes and the oddest sensation hit her. Everything inside her went still. It was as if time stopped.

12

"She'll be answering your questions."

The professor's voice started time moving forward again. Erin gave herself a mental shake and drew in a breath of air. "Hello, Mr. Carlson." She smiled and extended her hand. It was swallowed by his larger one. Warmth telegraphed itself up her arm. She glanced at their joined hands, shocked by the feeling.

"A pleasure, Ms. Kelly."

A manila folder smacked down on the only clean spot on the desk. Erin jumped, withdrew her hand from the encompassing warmth and focused her fragmented attention as Professor Stiles fastened a keen-eyed look on David Carlson.

"Erin knows as much about the grant as I do, young man, and she's better at tolerating questions about our operation." He slapped his hand down on the folder. "This is a copy of the grant for reference — I don't want any misquotes." He looked at her.

"You can tell him about the center, Erin."

"But — ?"

A wave of her boss's hand cut her off. "I've no time to discuss the matter, I'm already late for another appointment. I'll talk with you later." He grabbed up his suit jacket and rushed from the room.

Erin could have cheerfully shaken him.

The least he could have done was warn her! She snatched up the folder, clasped it to her chest and turned around. "Well, Mr. Carlson, it looks as if you're stuck with me for your interview. I'll do my best to answer your questions, but — as you've probably guessed — I'm surprised by this assignment and therefore ill-prepared."

"That makes two of us that are surprised, Ms. Kelly." David Carlson's gaze lowered to her hands holding the file.

Erin's breath caught. He was checking for a ring. A *Romeo?* Her caution reflexes snapped into high gear.

His gaze lifted back up to meet hers and he smiled. "And, speaking for myself, very pleasantly surprised. I'll take dining with a lovely young lady rather than an irascible old man every time."

Smooth, Mr. Carlson, very smooth — but then practice makes perfect. Disappointment filtered through the remnant of that odd stillness. "Dining?"

David Carlson's smile spread into a slow grin. "It's a luncheon appointment."

David felt like he'd taken a hard right to the stomach. The punch had landed when he'd first looked down into Erin Kelly's big, dark-green eyes, and it left him taut-

14

muscled and breathless.

David frowned, motioned to the busy hostess and, at her nod, guided Erin to his favorite table at Carlo's Villa. He'd been looking forward to a plate of chicken marsala — now he wasn't sure he could eat. His appetite was gone. All he really wanted was to run his fingers through the smooth, thick mass of hair framing Erin Kelly's lovely face. Her hair was the deep red-brown color of the chili powder in his kitchen cupboard.

"Thank you." Erin smiled up at him and slid onto the chair he held for her.

David's fingers tightened on the top rail. Her smile had the same effect as her beautiful eyes. He nodded, cleared his throat and went to take his own seat.

"Good afternoon, Mr. Carlson." The server placed a glass of ice water trimmed with twin slices of lemon and lime in front of each of them, then laid dark-blue menus edged with gold on the burgundy-and-gray striped tablecloth. "Would you care for something to drink while you decide on your meals? Perhaps a light wine?"

"Erin?"

"No, thank you. The water is fine for me."

David gave a mental *whew!* He was close to punch drunk from looking at her. He didn't need alcohol. "I'll have a lemonade."

"Very good, sir. I'll be back with it shortly."

David glanced at his menu, then pushed it aside and feasted on the sight of Erin studying hers. She lifted her head and caught him watching her. Her eyes clouded. *So she was wary of being interviewed.*

"Have you decided?"

Her hair shimmered in the light streaming through the window as she nodded. She looked down and closed her menu. When she looked up, the shadow in her eyes was gone. "I'll have antipasto . . . and bread sticks." She gave a rueful smile. "I can't resist their bread sticks."

David grinned. "I know what you mean." He leaned back against his chair and set himself to put her at ease. "So, Erin Kelly, what part of Ireland are your ancestors from?"

She gave a little shrug. "I don't know. That information was never passed on." She smiled and reached for her glass. "I have a suspicion the earliest Kelly to reach America's shores didn't want that knowledge made public."

"Aha! Skeletons!" David rubbed his hands together.

Erin laughed. "Careful. Your reporter

radar is showing." She took a swallow of water and put her glass down. "What about you? Where do your people come from?"

"I have no idea. I'm just glad they had the good sense to come here."

"Amen to that."

She sounded sincere and utterly natural. Was she religious? David's smile faded. It was the first flat note struck since he'd met her.

"Your lemonade, Mr. Carlson." The server placed it in front of him, then gathered the menus under his arm. "And your order?"

David glanced at Erin. She nodded. He looked back at the server. "We'll have the antipasto tray with choice of dressings on the side. Bread sticks —" he smiled "— double up on the bread sticks. And minestrone for me. Erin?" She held up her hand with the thumb and forefinger only an inch or so apart. He nodded. "Make that two minestrones — one large, one small."

"Very good, sir." The server hurried away.

David took a swallow of his drink, then put down his glass and leaned forward. "Professor Stiles seems like quite a character. Do you enjoy working with him?" Her face warmed. It was the only way he could describe it. He knew before she spoke she admired Robert Stiles.

17

"Yes, I do. Very much. I know he seems rather a cliché character — you know, rough exterior, heart of gold — but in his case it's absolutely true. He started the center, and he fights like a lion when anyone threatens to stop funding the literacy program. Our slogan is When You Open A Book, You Open The World. That's why this grant is so important. You have no idea how many adults there are who cannot read or write — or do so at a minimal level."

She looked fully into his eyes, and for a moment he lost the thread of the conversation.

"— and when a person can read and write their possibilities are *endless*. At the center we see these adults go from hopeless to hopeful." Suddenly she stopped. "I'm sorry, Mr. Carlson. I didn't mean to make a speech."

David put on a mock frown. "That's David, remember? We agreed on that earlier. But, to get back to the point — please don't apologize. I like people who are passionate about the things they believe in." He gave her his most charming smile. "I think there's a little of the lion in you, too, when it comes to the literacy program."

"Perhaps so. It's very important to me."

David stared at her, taken aback by the

quiet acknowledgment. He wasn't accustomed to having his openings for a little flirting ignored. He took another tack. "Professor Stiles said you were the program coordinator. I'm not familiar with the way the program is set up. Is that a paid position?"

"It will be starting in July — thanks to the grant. At the moment no one in the program is salaried. It's all volunteer. Our funds have been used only for needed teaching supplies."

"What about rent?"

"Professor Stiles owns the building we use and he doesn't take a dime for rent. He even pays the taxes out of his own pocket." Affection warmed her smile. "I told you he has a heart of gold."

Or a comfortable tax writeoff. That would have to be investigated. David took another swallow of lemonade, then leaned back out of the way while the server returned and placed their food on the table. When the man left, David laid his napkin over his leg, filled his plate from the antipasto tray and drizzled dressing over it. "I know Professor Stiles works at the university, but what about you, Erin? Since you've been volunteering all your time and talent, you must be one of the idle rich."

Her laughter sounded like music.

"I'm afraid not." She looked up from fixing her plate. "I've only been able to volunteer at Westwood a few evenings a week. But that will all change now. School will be out in three weeks, and I'll begin full-time work at the center."

"School?" David lifted the wicker basket, folded back the napkin and held the basket out to Erin. "You're a teacher?"

She nodded, took a bread stick and broke it in half before putting it on her bread plate. "I teach kindergarten at Living Hope Christian School."

The moment turned sour — not to mention his stomach. "I'm sure that's very rewarding." It was a lame response, but it was the best he could dredge up.

"Yes, it is." She gave him a long, measuring look, then bowed her head.

She was saying grace! David resisted the urge to get up and walk away. He set the basket down, sliced off a bite of prosciutto, stabbed it with his fork, then added a sliver of green pepper and began to eat.

Erin lifted her head and their gazes met. David ignored the reactive quickening of his pulse and turned all business. He wanted to wrap up this interview, say goodbye and bolt out the door. It was a good thing she

20

had insisted on driving her own car — they could go their separate ways when the meal was over. "I think I'll find enough general information about the center in the brochure you gave me, Erin. Why don't you tell me about the grant."

Erin opened her car door, then turned and swept her gaze over the stucco and beam exterior of Carlo's Villa. She wasn't used to eating leisurely business lunches in fancy restaurants — she belonged to the "grab a sandwich and get back to work" crowd. And that's exactly what she needed to do — get back to work.

Erin slid into the driver's seat, secured her seatbelt, switched on the ignition and looked in the rearview mirror. A man and woman, standing beside a car in the row directly behind her, were locked in a passionate kiss. The man ran his hand over the woman's body, pressing her close against him.

Erin jerked her gaze away, shifted into Reverse and looked over her shoulder as she backed out. The man stopped whatever he was doing to the woman's neck and lifted his head to glance toward the moving vehicle.

Jerry!

Erin gasped. Of its own volition, her foot jammed on the brakes and the car jolted to a stop. The woman turned her head to look. *Dr. Swan's new receptionist!*

Erin's stomach knotted. She whipped around to face front, locking her gaze on the mirror. Jerry mouthed something to the young woman, and they resumed their embrace with increased ardor. Erin swallowed back a surge of nausea, shifted gears and drove away. All thought of her pleasant lunch disappeared as a wave of anger washed over her at seeing her sister's live-in boyfriend with another woman.

CHAPTER TWO

"You were off your game big-time tonight, Dave. The 'Tiger' didn't show up, you were more like a pussycat."

David yanked the towel from around his neck, scrubbed it over his still damp hair and glanced at Ted. "Is that right?"

"It sure is." Ted jammed his own towel in his duffel bag. "Your concentration was way off. What's up?"

"Nothing. I just had a bad night."

"Yeah, right. That excuse might work for mere mortals, but you, my friend —" David braced himself for the solid thump that hit his shoulder "— you need a better reason. Anything I can help with?"

"Nope." David pulled his T-shirt on and stuffed it into his jeans. "Not unless you've turned into an expert on women."

"Oh?" Ted's eyebrows raised, a grin spread across his face. "*You're* asking *me* for advice about women? How the mighty are fallen!"

He rubbed his hands together. "I'm going to enjoy this! So spill it. Just what is the difficulty between you and the illustrious model?"

David shot him a look. "Her name is Brandee. And she's not the problem. I met a woman I can't get out of my mind, that's all. Hence my lack of concentration —" he thumped Ted back "— and your bogus win."

"That's as good an excuse as any." Ted's grin slipped into a frown. "I thought you and Brandee only dated for mutual professional benefit — that you were each free to see others."

"True."

"So what's the problem?" Ted leveled his "lawyer look" on him. "Why don't you just call this other woman? Is she married?"

"No." David scowled. "She's religious."

"Ouch!"

He nodded. "My feelings exactly. Now it's time for me to go home and put the finishing touches on tomorrow's column. Why don't you go chase an ambulance and drum up some legal business? Unless you want to get a pizza or something?"

Ted's grin returned. "No can do, Tiger. I'm booked for the night. And believe me, when I leave here, it isn't an ambulance I'll be chasing after."

David laughed and crammed his playing clothes in his gym bag along with his damp towel. "How *is* Darlene?"

Ted zipped his bag. "Fantastic! I proposed last Saturday."

"Wow! I didn't see that one coming." David lifted out his shoes and slammed his locker door. He turned and stared at his lifelong friend. "What happened to 'Mr. Confirmed Bachelor'?"

Ted laughed. "He took one look at Darlene and died a sudden death. When it's right — it's right." He sobered. "There's no way I can fight what I feel for her, Dave. I don't even want to try."

"That's great, Ted." David stuck out his hand. "Congratulations."

"Yeah. Thanks." Ted shook hands, then shifted his stance. "Looks like it's going to be a no-holds-barred wedding. Will you be best man?"

David gave him a crooked grin. "What do you mean, 'will I be'? I always have been."

Ted snorted. "Not in Darlene's eyes — and that's all that matters." He picked up his bag and headed for the door. "I'll tell her you said yes and she can scratch you off the 'things to be done for the wedding' list." He pulled open the door, stepped outside, then hesitated. "See you next Wednesday.

And make sure the 'Tiger' shows up, okay? I like a little competition."

David threw his shoe at him. He wasn't quick enough. The shoe crashed against the closed door. He grinned, grabbed his other shoe and cocked his arm. He didn't have long to wait. The door eased open and Ted stuck his head through the crack. David let the shoe fly.

"Whoa!"

Ted's head disappeared behind the door. The shoe sailed through the narrow opening into the hallway. David laughed. *Not a bad shot.*

A moment later the door opened wide and a grinning Ted tossed his shoe back to him. "Told you you're off your game tonight, pal. That woman must really be something!" The door closed on his laughter.

David shook his head, retrieved his other shoe and sat on the bench to put them on. Erin Kelly *was* "really something," but not for him. He frowned and shifted his thoughts to his friend. Ted *married!*

David gave a disbelieving snort, zipped his bag and left the locker room. He might have been off his game, but he'd worked up an appetite just the same.

"The penny glee . . . aaams."

"Not quite, Amber." Erin smiled at the teenager sitting beside her. "Remember the rule. When there are two vowels, the first vowel says its own name and the second vowel is silent."

The girl nodded her head, then bent forward over the children's reading book. Her forehead furrowed in concentration. "The penny glee . . . mmms. Gleems!"

"That's right! Good job, Amber." Erin's heart swelled as the teenager lifted her head and smiled. "Friday night we'll start a new book." Erin smiled encouragement. "You'll be reading and writing with the best of us in no time. I promise."

The tension in the girl's face eased. She nodded, and rose to her feet. "I hope so. I need to learn to read so I can get a better job. Doing dishes in a restaurant doesn't pay enough to live on, and I'll be on my own when I graduate this month. I don't know what good school did me!" She shrugged and tugged her purse strap over her shoulder. "Thanks for your help, Miss Kelly. I'll see you Friday."

"You're welcome, Amber. Good night." Erin picked up the child's reading book they'd been using and carried it to the cupboard.

"Miss Kelly? Will you help me with this

27

word? I don't think it obeys the rules you taught me."

Erin turned and smiled at the frustrated fourteen-year-old. "Sometimes words don't obey rules, Janine. Let me see. Oh. You can do this one." She put her hand on the teenager's shoulder urging her forward. "Let's go sit at the table and I'll help you figure it out."

Almost ten o'clock. Another long day. And she still had papers to correct. Erin dropped her shoulder bag on the couch, slid her feet out of her pumps and wiggled her toes into the carpet. *Wonderful!* What *was* it about taking your shoes off? She could almost purr.

Erin reached for the TV remote resting on the coffee table beside the framed picture of Alayne she'd requested for her birthday a few weeks ago. She picked up the picture and studied her sister's face. Alayne was smiling in the photograph, but there was unhappiness in her eyes. Did she know about Jerry's affair?

Erin frowned. If only she could talk with Alayne about it. If only she could talk to their mom and dad about it! But that was out of the question. The familiar sadness swept through her. Erin sighed, put down the picture, picked up the remote and clicked on the TV. All she could do was wait and make herself available.

Piano music filled the room. Erin sank down onto the couch closing her eyes as a voice started touting a concert in the city. What would it feel like to play like that?

"A *Channel Four News* exclusive! This is Robert Sheffield reporting live. Only minutes ago there was a shooting here on Humbard Street —"

Erin opened her eyes. The flashing lights of an ambulance and two police cars blinked behind the man on her TV screen.

"— We've been unable to talk with police and obtain details as yet, but initial reports place two witnesses on the scene at the time of the shooting. And as you can see . . ." The reporter stepped aside, giving a graphic description of the scene while the TV camera panned to the sidewalk across the street. Two men knelt beside a body.

"Ugh! Sorry, Robert Sheffield, but this is nothing I want to see." Erin reached for the remote, then stopped when she caught sight of two men standing with a policeman in a darkened doorway in the background. Poor men. They must be the eyewitnesses. What a horrible experience!

A flash of brilliance from the rotating light

of the ambulance swept across the recessed entrance highlighting the men's faces for a moment and Erin jerked forward. *That was David Carlson!* She stared at the man on the left. She must be wrong about the witness thing. He was probably just covering the story for *The Herald.* But he wasn't talking to anyone. He was just standing there. She leaned closer to the TV, watching David.

Suddenly a hand appeared, and the screen went black. A voice, obviously connected to the hand covering the lens, ordered someone to turn the camera off. There was an indistinguishable mumble in reply, and a moment later the hand was removed, revealing the reporter standing in front of the *Channel Four News* van. "This concludes our live coverage at this time. We'll have updates as details become avail—"

Erin snatched up the remote, clicked the TV off and leaned back against the couch. David Carlson. She had enjoyed the time she spent with him, which was unusual because she was always so tense around men. It was probably his professional interviewing skills that had made her relax. Of course, it helped that his behavior had been impeccable. He'd been polite and nice. And he was so intelligent.

Erin bent down, scooped up her shoes and

headed upstairs to change into comfortable clothes. Why was she thinking about how nice David Carlson seemed? She'd never see him again — except occasionally on TV. She pursed her lips in speculation. She could be wrong, but it sure looked as if he'd witnessed that shooting. For his sake she hoped not.

David unlocked his door and stepped into his entrance hall. The leather globe light, suspended from the plastered ceiling, shone onto the objects atop the red-lacquered chest below it. He dropped his keys into the brass bowl, then tugged his necktie loose and moved down the two steps into the living room.

It had been quite a day. Witnessing that shooting had shaken him more than he cared to admit. He'd never seen a man's life snuffed out in the space of a moment before. He'd almost lost his dinner. And then there was the police questioning, and his own limited account of the story to write for the paper. Too bad he had to report in general terms. This story could have been his big break. Maybe it still could be.

David rotated the tension from his neck and shoulders, then flipped the switch that turned on the indirect lighting and punched the button on his answering machine.

"David, darling? Are you there? It's after eight." A tiny bit of impatience crept into Brandee Rogers's honeyed tones. "I thought you'd be home by now. Even reporters — Oh, never mind. I'm calling because I want you to take me to Charlene's this Saturday night. She's having one of her fabulous spur-of-the-moment parties, and you know everyone who is anyone in town will be trying to wrangle an invitation. I happened to run into her at lunch today so I'm in. And so are you, darling. She made a point of mentioning you. I'm jealous."

David frowned at the coy words and tone. He could almost see Brandee's full lower lip sticking out in an affected pout. She was getting a little too possessive. Maybe he should call a halt to —

"Call me, darling, and I'll give you all the particulars." She gave a throaty laugh. "Well, maybe not all of them. Wait until you see me in my new dress. Byeeee."

Or maybe not. David lifted his hand and rubbed the muscles at the nape of his neck. Brandee might be using him to polish up her social image, but it didn't do his prestige any harm to have a beautiful model draped on his arm either. And you never knew who would show up at Charlene's parties. She definitely traveled with the high crowd. Saturday night was a must. So why didn't he feel his usual enthusiasm? Was it because he couldn't get a cloud of dark red hair and a pair of beautiful green eyes out of his mind? Let alone the power-packed smile that went with them.

David frowned, leaped the two steps up into the kitchen and pulled open the refrigerator door. He hadn't been able to get Erin Kelly out of his mind all week. She'd even cost him his Wednesday night handball game with Ted.

David scowled and poured himself a glass of orange juice. He'd dated quite a few women, but none of them had attached themselves so firmly to his thoughts that he couldn't concentrate. That had never happened before.

When it's right — it's right.

Ted's words set his teeth on edge. "Buddy, you don't know what you're talking about. Erin Kelly is definitely not right for me. So you and Ms. Kelly can *both* get out of my head!"

David guzzled the orange juice, rinsed the glass, then stuck it in the dishwasher and grabbed the handset from the kitchen phone. He was in a lousy mood tonight, but he knew the cure. He pushed a button with his thumb.

"Hello?"

That breathy thing she did with her voice suddenly seemed irritating. He scowled. "Hello, Brandee."

"David, darling! You got my message?"

"Yes. That's why I'm calling." David put his odd mood down to the residue of emotion left over from the shooting and forced a light note into his voice. "I'm looking forward to seeing you in that dress Saturday night."

CHAPTER THREE

Erin frowned down at the paper she was correcting, glanced at the little boy in the third row and pursed her lips. There had to be a reason for the error, he was one of her brightest students. He never made a mistake when it came to choosing the correct vowel to make a word. "Michael, would you come here for a moment please?"

The blond head lifted instantly. The five-year-old put down his pencil and hurried up to her desk. She motioned for him to come stand beside her. "Michael, this is your paper. Would you read the word with the vowel you've chosen please?"

"Buke."

"And what would it be with the other vowel choice?"

"Bike."

"That's right. Now, which one do you want to choose?"

"Buke."

Erin studied Michael's face for a moment. He was dead serious. Why would he choose the *u* instead of the *i?* "Use *buke* in a sentence, Michael."

"When I'm bad, my daddy bukes me."

Ah! Erin fought back a grin. "That's *re-*bukes, Michael. When you're bad, your daddy rebukes you."

"Oh." Michael's little blond eyebrows drew together and he pointed at the paper. "Then that's wrong. Can I change it?"

"*May* I change it?" Erin gave him a hug. "Yes, you may." She handed him the paper. "Bring it back when you've corrected it." She watched Michael scurry back to his desk, then rose and hurried from the room as her suppressed mirth threatened to break free.

"Erin?"

She glanced toward the office. Betty Fowler motioned her to come in. "You have a telephone call."

David slipped his cell phone into his suit coat pocket. That was that. Erin Kelly would meet him at the Oak Street Diner at four-thirty to answer the rest of his questions about Professor Stiles's literacy program. Too bad all the people he had to interview for stories weren't that polite, pleasant or accommodating. Or soft spoken. A smile curved his lips. Erin Kelly had a great voice. And fantastic looks. Those eyes of hers —

Hold up, buddy! Don't travel down that road. It doesn't matter how attractive or nice Erin Kelly is — she's not for you. Not with that religious baggage she's carrying around!

David shook his head, checked traffic and ran across Bartlett Street to Domingo's. Given the strength of his attraction to Erin Kelly, it was a good thing he'd only asked her to meet him for coffee. Twenty minutes tops, and he'd be out of there. Then he'd never see Erin Kelly again. But that was later. Right now he had a few questions to ask Danny Arcano about that shooting the other night. Danny always knew the talk on the streets.

David focused his attention on the job at hand, shoved open the door of the bar and stepped into the dark interior.

No matter how Erin tried to calm herself, nerves flittered in her stomach. She knew she was being silly. This wasn't personal. David Carlson only wanted to ask her some questions. Still . . . the flitters increased.

Erin scowled, took a quick peek in the visor mirror and pushed her hair back behind her ears. It didn't help much, but without a comb it would have to do. Why didn't she carry a purse like other women! She stared at the pink her nervous tension brought to her cheeks and wrinkled her nose in distaste. At least she didn't have to worry about being pale. She looked like a clown.

Erin flipped the visor up in disgust, reached into the ashtray for the lip balm she used to keep her lips soft and moist and spread it on. Maybe she should use it on her tongue, too — her mouth was so dry she could hardly swallow. *Relax! You handled the first interview well.*

She gave an unladylike snort. Like that was the reason she was tense! It was the thought of David Carlson that made her nervous. She'd never reacted to a man the way she had to him. When their gazes had met that first time, and he'd taken hold of her hand —

Okay. Enough of the foolishness! She was ready. Erin glanced down at her melon-colored jacket dress, sighed and climbed from the car. Why hadn't she worn her new, flax-colored suit today, which made her look older, more professional? Because she didn't know David Carlson would call and ask her to meet him for coffee after work.

And there went those flitters again. *Stop it! It's only a business appointment.* Erin frowned, crossed the parking lot and reached for the chrome bar on the diner's blue-painted door as she stepped into the canopied entrance.

"Allow me."

Erin jerked sideways and glanced up straight into David Carlson's smiling face. He must have been waiting for her. Had he seen her primping in the car? She turned away as the telltale warmth of embarrassment crept into her cheeks. *So much for presenting a professional demeanor.*

"A dollar for your thoughts." David reached around in front of her and pulled the door open.

"A dollar?" Erin stepped into the diner. "That's generous of you." She slanted a look at him. "Last I knew, thoughts were only worth a penny."

"Inflation." David followed her inside. "Besides, you looked so serious, your thoughts are probably worth more than a dollar." He ushered her to a booth by a window. "Did you have a hard day at work?"

Erin shook her head and slid onto the red vinyl bench seat. "I never have a hard day. I love my job. The children are wonderful." She looked over at him, feeling more at ease with the width of the aluminum-edged table between them. "How about you?"

"Well, I can't say I never have a hard day." His lips twisted into a wry smile. "Not everyone appreciates the job I do. In fact some of them get downright nasty when I'm investigating a story they're involved in. But, like you, I love my work — in spite of the rough situations I occasionally encounter."

"Are you ready to order?"

Order? We just sat down! Erin glanced up at the young server. The teenager was staring at David and practically drooling on her order pad. So that was it. Well, she could certainly understand. David Carlson was hands down the most handsome man she'd ever seen. She cleared her throat to get the girl's attention. "I'll have an unsweetened iced tea with lemon, please." The girl's gaze didn't so much as flicker in her direction. She might as well have been mute and invisible.

"Make mine coffee — hot and black."

The girl smiled at David and wrote it down. "Is that all? Are you sure there's nothing else I can get for you? The menu's there on the table." She gestured, but didn't take her eyes off David. "I'll wait if you need more time."

The girl was all but cooing at him! Erin ducked her head and stared down at her lap, freeing David to respond to the teenager's blatant flirting, if he so chose.

"Only the coffee and iced tea with lemon, thank you."

Out of the corner of her eye, Erin watched the server walk over to the counter, hips swinging seductively.

"You can come up for air now."

So he'd been aware of what she was doing! She lifted her head and met David's gaze head-on.

"I'm sorry, Erin, that was awkward." His lips tilted in a rueful smile. "She's young."

He sounded kind and a tiny bit embarrassed, which — she knew perfectly well — meant absolutely nothing. Men were such liars. She gave him a cool look. "Yes, she is. Anyway, it's over — until she comes back."

David folded his arms across his chest, relaxed back against the seat and fastened his gaze on her. "That sounds a little skeptical. I'm surprised. Cynicism doesn't fit you, Erin." He shifted his position toward her and lowered his voice. "You don't think I'm going to respond to her flirting, do you? She must be ten years my junior!"

That doesn't stop Jerry! Erin's skin prickled with anger. She yanked her thoughts back to David. "I have a sinister side to my nature."

"Sinister? If you think that's sinister, you

41

need to read the newspaper more often."
He sat back and grinned. "I can recommend
a good column."

His grin was contagious. Erin smiled in
response, then reached up to tuck the hair
that had swung free back behind her ear.
Professional, remember? Keep it professional.
"Speaking of your column — you had some
questions you wanted to ask me?"

David's eyebrows rose. He stared across
the table at her, and the intensity of his
scrutiny made her want to get up and walk
away. After a moment, his lips spread in a
smile that trapped the breath in her lungs.
"Business only, huh? You're an enigma, Erin
Kelly. But I'm not an investigative reporter
for nothing. I'll figure you out. Now, about
the questions."

Erin's breath released a gust of relief as
David shifted gears. She could hold her own
with the reporter side of him — it was the
man that knocked her off-kilter.

"When we first talked about the center,
Erin, you said I would be surprised at the
number of adults that can't read — or
words to that effect. Are there really that
many?"

She gave an emphatic nod, relieved to be
on solid professional ground. "The number
is shocking. And I can't tell you the nega-

tive impact it has on their lives! They get stuck in low-paying jobs, which often leads to less-than-desirable low-income housing options. And, even then they have to accept help from the state simply to buy groceries. Their self-esteem suffers and —"

David's lips curved upward.

Erin stiffened. "You find that amusing?"

He shook his head. "No. I find that disturbing. But I also find myself admiring your wrath on behalf of the center's clients and those sparks of anger flashing in your dark green eyes." His gaze locked on hers. "You really are passionate about this problem."

Thankfully, the server chose that moment to bring their drinks, because Erin couldn't speak. Her numb-struck mind couldn't think of an adequate reply. It had stalled on the fact that David Carlson said he admired her, and the altogether foolish and inappropriate response of her wildly fluttering heart.

Erin frowned at the ringing phone. This was the third call. She was never going to get these papers graded by tomorrow! She dropped her pen and lifted the handset. "Hello?"

"Hi, Boots! Where were you? I tried to get

hold of you after work."

The dilemma she'd been struggling with ever since she'd witnessed Jerry's infidelity hit Erin full force at the sound of her sister's voice. She sagged back into her favorite overstuffed chair, burning with the desire to tell Alayne about Jerry's behavior, and certain it would only widen the chasm in their family if she did. "Sorry, Alayne. I had coffee with David Carlson at that little diner on Oak Street, then grabbed some pizza and went straight to the center. What did you want?" *She must know. The receptionist works in the same office!*

"Who *cares?*" Excitement sizzled out of the phone. "You had coffee with David Carlson the reporter? The one who's on *Channel Four News* every once in awhile? Way to go, Erin! That guy's *scrumptious!* And he's on his way up, too." Her older sister's voice was flooded with admiration. "Not only is he great at his job, but from all I hear, he knows how to play the 'climbing the social ladder to success' game with the best of them. So, what's he like?"

Erin pushed aside her dilemma and focused on the conversation. "He's intelligent. And polite and charming." *Far too charming!* "And funny — in a nice sort of way, nothing off-color or suggestive."

"He sounds perfect for you. Did he ask you out again?"

Erin let out an exasperated sigh. "He didn't ask me out this time. It wasn't a *date,* Alayne. He just had some questions about the literacy program. He's going to do a story about the center for his features column. You know, the long column that runs every Saturday."

"My mistake. Sorry, Boots. I thought maybe you had finally — Never mind. It's probably just as well it wasn't a date." Alayne's voice took on a protective tone. "David Carlson is a lady-killer for sure. And he's no —"

Erin winced as her sister chopped off her words. "No what?"

"No . . . choir boy. Not that I've heard anything bad about him, but you're not used to moving in his circles, you'd be no match for him. Look, I've got to go, Boots. We're at the club and Jerry's pulling into a parking place. I'll be in touch. Bye."

The phone went dead.

"Alayne, you're so *blind!*" Erin dropped the handset onto the cushion and surged to her feet. Nothing had changed. Alayne still thought being a Christian made you weak and vulnerable. Well, *she* would never become involved with a lying, cheating

45

woman chaser like Jerry! And that included David Carlson!

Lady-killer. She could believe that from the way he had handed her that smooth line about "sparks" in her dark-green eyes! *Sparks. Hah!*

Erin stalked out to the mirror above the chest in the entrance hall, switched on the lamp and studied her reflection. Her eyes were an unusual dark green — almost the color of the leaves on the rhododendron bush by her front walk — but there were no "sparks" in them. That was just a sample of the glib compliments handed out by men to disarm woman. She knew that. So why was she staring in the mirror?

Erin turned away in disgust. *No choir boy . . . you'd be no match for him.* That was ridiculous! David Carlson may be the most handsome and charming man she'd ever met, but she didn't trust him any more than any other man. She'd learned the folly of trusting a man — even seemingly nice, respectable ones — seven years ago. After all, Mr. Gorseman had been one of the best liked teachers in high school.

I'm sure you did the experiment, Erin, but, unfortunately, it's missing. Meet me in the lab after school and I'll let you repeat it.

A chill chased down Erin's spine. How

naive and trusting she'd been then. She'd believed Mr. Gorseman's lie and gone in all innocence to meet him. And if Alayne — who came looking for her — hadn't heard a noise and looked in the window of the locked and darkened science room to see Mr. Gorseman poised atop her on the lab table, he would have succeeded in his plan to rape her. And she — unconscious from the drug he'd put in the soda he'd given her — would never have known exactly what happened or who did it.

A deep shudder shook her. Erin wrapped her arms about herself and leaned against the chest, waiting for the reaction to pass. If only he'd been found guilty. But he'd lied his way out of it. At the inquiry, he denied her charge and explained her unconscious state by saying she'd been careless in handling the noxious chemicals in the experiment and had been overcome by fumes. He refuted Alayne's charge by saying she was mistaken and overwrought, that he'd been trying to *help* Erin when Alayne started beating on the door. And he explained the locked door away by saying she, Erin, had a "crush" on him and must have locked it so they would be alone. It was his lies against their truth — and he was a beloved and respected teacher. All charges had been dropped.

Erin's hands tightened around her upper arms, digging her fingertips into the soft flesh. It was that experience that had destroyed Alayne's trust in God and ultimately split their family. It was the reason she, herself, was so wary and distrustful of men that she'd never been able to have a successful relationship.

Erin frowned and walked back into the living room. She didn't want to be that way. She wanted to fall in love and marry and have children. She'd even dated a few times. But when a man showed interest in becoming close, when he tried to hold her or kiss her, she panicked, her defenses kicked in and she stopped seeing him. She knew it was foolish, but she couldn't help herself.

Erin sighed, sat down in the chair and picked up her pen to finish grading the papers. Maybe someday she would find a man she could trust and fall in love with, but it wouldn't be a "lady-killer" like David Carlson. No matter how he made her feel!

David opened the folder, stared down at the phone number he'd scrawled on the inside of the cover then closed it again. Was it too late to call? He checked his watch. It wasn't quite eleven. He reached for the portable phone, then drew his hand back and walked away from his desk. It didn't matter what time it was — no time would be the right time to call Erin Kelly.

David scowled and scrubbed his hands through his hair. "Get out of my head, woman! I'm not calling you now or ever!"

He walked over to the window and stared out into the night feeling edgy and aggravated. Just the thought of religion had that effect on him. He'd had enough of it from his missionary father to last him a lifetime. He knew what it felt like to be ignored and unwanted by a religious zealot. He'd lived his life that way. He didn't need that from anyone else — certainly not a woman. So why couldn't he forget about Erin Kelly? Why did she stick like a burr to his consciousness?

"Aaah!" David strode over to the door, snapped off the study lights then immediately flipped them back on when the phone rang. His pulse quickened as he strode to his desk. Maybe this was a breaking story. A *big* story. He snatched up the receiver. "David Carlson."

"I saw you on TV with that cop. Don't ID the shooter. Bad things happen to guys with big mouths."

"Who is — ?" The receiver went dead. David stared at it for a moment, debating calling the cops. But one thing he'd learned as a reporter — people got their kicks in strange ways. Like making crank calls. This guy was probably yet another of those wackos. And if the cops tapped his phone and his informants found out about it . . .

David hung up the receiver, turned off the lights again then headed for the kitchen to get a glass of juice before it was time to switch on the TV and watch the news. His lips curled into a smile as he jumped the two steps and walked to the refrigerator. Someday he would be the reporter holding the microphone and smiling into the camera. He was close to making that goal come true. He'd already made the right contacts. All he needed was that one big story!

CHAPTER FOUR

Hmm, let's see . . . poster boards, markers, letter stencils and tracing paper — that should do it. Now all she needed was some manila folders and she was finished shopping. Erin wheeled the cart down the next aisle, picked up the folders and headed for the checkout.

"Did you find everything you wanted to-day?"

"Yes, thank you." She smiled at the cashier and lifted the items out of the cart onto the counter.

"Cash or charge?"

"Charge." She reached into her pocket.

"Erin?"

David Carlson. Erin's pulse stuttered. It had been two weeks, but she'd know that rich, baritone voice anywhere. She arranged her features into a polite smile and turned. "Hello, Mr. Carlson."

"That's *David.*" He inclined his head toward the items the clerk was putting into

51

a plastic bag. "Looks like you've got a big project coming up."

"Yes." She handed the woman the school's credit card. "The children learned about animals from the different areas of our country this year, and we're going to make posters about them to decorate our room for graduation." She signed her name to the slip, then slid the card and the receipt in her jeans pocket.

"Sounds like fun."

"I think the children will enjoy it." She gave him a polite smile. "Nice seeing you again." She lifted the bag off the counter, and the large poster boards promptly flopped out onto the floor. "Oops!"

David stooped and picked up the boards. "Slippery things, plastic bags. I'll carry these for you."

"That's very kind, but —" she stretched out her hand "— I don't want to be a bother."

"No bother." David tucked the posters under his arm, paid for the ink cartridge he was buying and followed her out the door. "Where's your car?"

"Across the street. I like to walk in the park when I'm finished shopping." She hurried her steps.

"That sounds like a good idea. Would you

mind if I joined you?"

Did he think — ? Erin jerked her head sideways to look at him. She'd disabuse him of *that* notion right now! "You don't have to do that. I wasn't *hinting.* I really *do* walk in the park whenever I come shopping." She stopped beside her car and pushed the button on her key to unlock the trunk.

"I believe you." David smiled down at her. "And even if you were hinting, I wouldn't have asked to join you unless I wanted to." His smile spread into a slow grin that paralyzed her lungs. "I was going to call and tell you I've finished the piece about the center and the new grant, but this way I get to tell you in person. The piece will be in the paper this Saturday."

"Wonderful! Professor Stiles will be so pleased." Erin put her shopping bag into the trunk. *All right, Mr. Carlson, message received! You can take your charming grin and leave any time now, so I can start breathing normally again.*

"Aha! What's this I see? A word game?" David picked up the box he'd moved aside to make room for the poster boards.

Erin nodded. "I play it with the children. You'd be surprised at how quickly a five-year-old can catch on to the concept of crosswords." She busied herself tying the

53

handles of the plastic bag together so she wouldn't have to look at him.

"I'll bet you always win."

"Well, of course I would if we played that way!" Erin shot David an annoyed look. *What sort of teacher did he think she was pitting her wisdom against the children's?* He was grinning again. Hot blood swamped her cheeks. He'd been teasing her — and she'd risen to the bait. His grin widened when their gazes met and she went breathless again. *Where was a paper bag when you needed one!*

"How are you against someone your own age?"

"I beg your pardon?" *He couldn't mean —*

"I challenge you to a game. Right here and now — on that table in the park." David pointed. "But before you accept, remember — I'm a reporter. Words are my business. I *never* lose at word games."

"Oh no?" Erin's lungs started to function correctly. *This* she could handle! She smiled. "I believe you may have just opened yourself up for your first loss, Mr. Carlson."

His eyes crinkled with amusement. "Because I'll be playing against you?" He reached out and gripped the trunk lid with his free hand.

Erin shook her head. "No. Because God's

word says, 'Pride goeth before destruction,' and that warning you gave me sounded suspiciously like pride to me."

"I see." David studied her for a moment, then gave the box he held a shake that rattled the tiles inside. "And *I* say, that you, Miss Kelly, do not know the difference between *pride* and *certainty.*"

"Really?" Erin tipped her head to the side and narrowed her eyes at him, relieved that, for whatever reason, his high-voltage grin had faded into a low-amp smile. "And *I* say, you're ready to take a tumble, Mr. Carlson. I accept your challenge."

"Good!" The trunk lid thudded down, emphasizing the word. "Have you eaten?"

Erin shook her head. "Not yet."

"Do you like subs?"

She nodded. "Yes, but —"

"Great!" He handed her the box. "You set up the game, while I run across the street and get a couple of subs — my treat. What's your pleasure?"

She stared at him a moment, then acquiesced. She *was* hungry. "A half ham and cheese — easy on the oil."

"Soda to drink?"

Not since Mr. Gorseman had drugged hers. She suppressed a shudder and shook her head. "I'll have coffee and a chocolate-chip

55

cookie."

David's grin returned. "A woman after my own taste buds! Okay, you've got it." He pivoted.

"Wait!" She gave him an apologetic smile when he turned back. "I forgot to tell you I want three creamers with the coffee."

"Three!" David gave her a look of absolute horror. "Are you sure you don't want me to get you a cup of milk and just have them toss a spoonful of coffee in it?"

She grinned at his teasing. "Don't be a coffee snob, David. I happen to like it that way. *Three* creamers."

He gave an exaggerated shudder. "All right. To each their own. But it's sacrilege."

Erin watched him jog across the road, then turned and headed for the picnic table, not quite certain what had just happened. David Carlson was too charming for her own good. He had breached her defensive walls. But one simple word game in a public park couldn't hurt.

"Ah, I've got one — *torose.*" David laid down his tiles. "Now, with the *s* added to *graze and* on a double-word square that will be forty-four points."

"Wait a minute!" Erin laughed and shook her head. "I've never heard of *torose.* Use it

56

in a sentence."

David raised his left eyebrow and gave her a diabolical grin. "Are you challenging me, Miss Kelly?"

She lifted both her hands into the air in a gesture of surrender. "I don't dare challenge you, Mr. Carlson. I learned my lesson on *retene.*" She gave a little laugh that reminded him of water flowing swiftly over rocks in a creek bed. "This request is for my edification only."

"In that case . . ." David made a manly effort to pull his thoughts back from Erin to the game. "The stem of many plants is torose in nature." He grinned. "That's *knobby* to the uninformed."

"Another new word learned for me — and another forty-four points earned for you." Erin gave a magnified sigh. "I can see if I ever want to win a game with you, I'm going to have to start reading the dictionary in my spare time." She jerked her gaze to his. "That was just a comment. I wasn't implying anything."

"I didn't think you were." David scanned her face. Tension had drawn the muscles taut. He smiled. "But it wouldn't bother me if you were. I always grant a rematch. It's only fair. I like to be a gracious winner."

His teasing had the desired effect. Erin

visibly relaxed and began to study the board. David studied her. What was it about the woman that undermined his determination to stay away from her? She wasn't tall and blond, or sophisticated and classically beautiful like the women he usually dated. Quite the opposite. She only came up to his chin. And right now, her dark-red hair was held up on the top of her head with one of those puffy fabric things Brandee wouldn't be caught dead in, and those little bits of hair that had popped free were driving him crazy!

David's fingers twitched. He pulled his gaze away from the errant tresses and took inventory of the rest of Erin's face. She had a sort of pert little nose. And great cheekbones. And her mouth . . . His went dry. It was dangerous to look at Erin's mouth. She wore no lipstick and her lips looked so soft and inviting —

"— be forty-two, thank you very much!"

David snapped back to attention. "I'm sorry?"

Erin pointed at the board. "*Squat* — on a triple-word square. That will be forty-two points please."

No extra long, fashionably painted nails. Just a nice, neat manicure. David picked up his pen and added her score. "That makes you twenty-seven points behind me." He gave her a lopsided grin. "Not exactly a commanding lead for me."

"Not exactly."

Her answering grin took him like a fist in the stomach — again. He wasn't sure he was going to survive many more such blows, but he couldn't think of a nicer way to expire. He also couldn't concentrate. He glanced at his tiles, then looked at the board. A drop of rain fell on the *z* in *blaze* and spattered across the checkered surface. Another fell. Then another.

"Uh-oh!" Erin reached for the box.

"I've got it." David jumped to his feet, scooped the tiles into the box then folded the board and slapped it on top. By the time he got the cover on, Erin had shoved the residue of their impromptu picnic into the paper bag.

Rain pelted down.

"Come on!" David darted around the table, grabbed Erin's free hand and ran toward the gazebo at the end of the path. When they arrived, his admiration for her took another giant leap upward. Her hair was wet, her clothes soaked and she was laughing. Brandee would have been screaming bloody murder! Not that she would have been playing a word game in the park in the first place. He felt a tug and lowered his gaze to their joined hands. He didn't want to, but he let go.

Erin turned and dropped the bag into the trash can beside the steps. "Well that's a first!" She shook her head, laughing as droplets of water flew everywhere. "I've never had a board game called because of rain."

"Nor I." David got lost somewhere in Erin's dark green eyes. "We *have* to have a rematch now. I don't want my reputation sullied by a questionable win."

She wrinkled her nose at him. "Anytime, Mr. Carlson. Anytime!"

David's hand clenched so hard the box popped. He put it down on the wide railing before he destroyed it.

"Where'd everyone go?" Erin glanced around. "Are we the only ones who took refuge here?"

David nodded. "I guess everyone else must have seen the rain coming and left."

"Smart people." She raised her hands and wrapped them about her bare upper arms. "I guess we were too involved in our game to notice the clouds rolling in."

"I guess." David frowned. She was shivering. "You're cold. I'm sorry I don't have a jacket to offer you, perhaps this will help."

He moved forward, folded his arms around her clasped ones and pulled her back against him. The moisture from the back of her sleeveless sweater penetrated his shirt front, momentarily cooling the skin on his chest. He took a breath, inhaling the suggestion of citrus that clung to her hair. His heart started thudding in time with the rain drumming on the roof. His grip tightened.

Erin went rigid, then shot from his grip like a bullet from a gun. He stared at her in astonishment.

"I'm all right now." She wrapped her arms around herself again and turned to look out at the park. "Do you like rain? I've always loved it. When I was young I used to beg my mother to let me go outside and walk around the yard just so I could listen to it beating on my umbrella. I still go for walks in the rain. And, I suppose it's silly, but I love to sit in a car when rain is pattering on the roof. Or on my back porch, so I hear it on the roof."

She was nervous! She was chattering like a magpie. At such an innocuous touch? David didn't know whether to be insulted or flattered. He put the debate aside until later. "I didn't enjoy rainstorms as a kid. They interfered with playing ball. But I did like riding my bike through the mud puddles afterward."

"Really?" Erin turned toward him. "And what did your mother think of that?"

He shook his head and leaned his shoulder against one of the roof support posts, blocking from his mind the feel of her in his arms. "My mom died when I was four years old."

"How awful. I'm sorry, David. I'm sure that was terribly hard for you."

The warmth and compassion in Erin's eyes and voice stirred his heart. He nodded. "Thanks. But it was a long time ago. It'll be twenty-four years next month."

"Do you have a stepmom?"

David straightened and jammed his hands in his jeans pockets, uncomfortable with talking about his personal life. "Yes. My father . . . does a lot of traveling." *For God.* Old anger snaked its way through him. "He met a woman overseas and remarried a few years later."

"So you moved a lot as a child?"

She sounded less nervous. David shook his head and skirted around the fact that his father and the new wife hadn't wanted him, because he would take time from their work for the Lord. "No. I lived with my grandmother and grandfather." He pulled up a smile. "Grandpa was a terrific gardener, and Grandma baked the best cookies in ten counties. As a matter of fact, you can blame Grandpa for those words I used in the game. I wanted to be like him, so I took up botany in college."

"Botany?" Those gorgeous eyes of hers widened in surprise. "How did you get from there to journalism?"

He shrugged. "One of my professors took me aside one day and told me I had an innate writing talent. He suggested I develop it and pursue fame and fortune as a journalist or writer. That sounded good to me, so I switched my major, and the rest, as they say, is history." He smiled. "Except in my case, history is still in the making."

"Now *that's* the sort of a teacher every child should have. Not the kind who only put in their time and totally ignore the needs of their students! Not the kind who —" Erin clamped her lips together and walked to the railing.

She was shivering again. David stayed rooted in place. He wasn't about to make the mistake of touching her again — no matter how innocent and altruistic his motives. "Sounds like you've had a bad experience with a teacher, Erin. Is that why you're so passionate about the literacy center?"

"Yes. It is."

He waited but she didn't expand on her

answer. She just stood there with her back toward him, staring out at the rain. Some emotion he felt but couldn't identify emanated from her. Pain? Anger? Whatever it was, he wanted to take her in his arms and comfort her, but that avenue was closed to him. He cleared his throat. "I'm sorry for whatever happened to you, Erin. But if that experience is what motivated your passion for helping your students at the center, at least some good has come out of it."

Her head lifted. She turned to look at him, then smiled. It felt as if someone had suddenly turned on the sun.

"Thank you, David." Her smile widened. "You're a very kind person —" she wrinkled her nose at him "— except when it comes to word games."

That little wrinkle of her nose stirred more than his heart. David dragged in a breath of air and returned her smile. "Kindness isn't in the rules."

Erin laughed, then shifted her gaze to the roof. "Listen. The rain has stopped. We can go home and dry out."

"I guess we can." David picked up the game and followed Erin down the steps, wishing — for the first time in his life — the deluge had continued.

■ ■ ■ ■

The rain had started again. Erin picked up her mug of hot cocoa, pushed open the back door and stepped out onto the porch. She was greeted by the steady drumming of raindrops on the roof overhead.

She took a deep breath, savoring the clean smell of the rain, then walked over to curl up in her favorite corner of the wicker couch. The cushion felt good against her bare feet. She snuggled them deeper into the softness and took a swallow of the cocoa, capturing one of the small marshmallows floating on top and letting its warm sweetness melt on her tongue.

If that experience is what motivated your passion for helping your students at the center, at least some good has come out of it.

Had her face revealed how startled she'd been by David's statement? Not only by his sensitivity, but by the truth he'd expressed. Erin wrapped both hands around the warm mug and stared out into the night. She'd lived so long with the legacy of distrust, fear and anger that Mr. Gorseman's attempted rape of her had caused, she'd never thought of the possibility of good coming from it. But it had. She'd become a teacher and a fierce advocate for the students at the literacy center because of it. And her mom and dad volunteered at the women's rape and abuse shelter as a result of her experience. But that was all for the good of others.

Erin set her cup on the table, rose and walked to the top of the steps, wrapping her arms about herself and leaning back against the support post to watch the raindrops dancing on the wet bricks of the walk. What about her? What about her family? Where was the good for them? All she'd received was an inability to trust a man. Alayne had turned her back on God and was living in sin with a lying, cheating lothario. And her parents suffered because their oldest daughter was too ashamed of the life she lived to even speak to them, and their youngest daughter was too wary of men to ever fall in love.

No, nothing good had come to them from that experience.

CHAPTER FIVE

Erin pulled the dress over her head, zipped up the back then eyed herself in the full-length mirror on the back of her closet door. She loved this sleeveless dress with its square-cut neckline and soft apricot-colored fabric that skimmed over her body before flaring to the flirty, lettuce-edge hem. It was so summery and feminine. And she definitely felt feminine. Ever since David put his arms around her Friday night she'd felt . . . well . . . womanly.

Erin scowled and lifted her hands to smooth the fabric covering her shoulders. What was wrong with her? She'd felt his heart thudding against her back. He'd wanted to kiss her. That he restrained himself didn't make him trustworthy, it only made him circumspect. They had been in an open gazebo in a public park with traffic passing by. It was the reason she hadn't totally panicked when he'd put his arms around her.

Erin stuck her tongue out at herself in the mirror. "Forget how nice David Carlson seems, Erin Kelly, and remember he has a reputation as a ladies' man! He wasn't interested in you. You were only with him because of an accidental meeting. He was just reacting according to form!"

Erin turned away from the mirror, stepped into her dress sandals and went to brush her hair. Her time would be better spent concentrating on the lesson she'd prepared for her Sunday school class.

"Who remembers how long it rained after Noah, his family and all the animals went into the ark?" Little hands shot up all around the room. Erin smiled. "Janie?"

"Forty days and forty nights."

"That's right. And who can tell me why God saved Noah and his family?" Erin swept her gaze over the class. "Andrew?"

" 'Cause Noah was the only one that was good. Everyone else was real bad!"

Erin nodded. "Yes. God's word tells us that only Noah walked with God. And *because* Noah walked with God, the Lord saved his whole family! And the Lord still does that today." She patted her Bible. "It says in God's word, 'Believe in the Lord

Jesus Christ, and thou shalt be saved — and thy house.' That means your family, not the house you live in."

Erin smiled and glanced at her watch. "Okay, that's all for today. I'll see you next week. You're dismissed." She rose and walked to the door. "Remember, no running." She stepped into the hall to watch the children walk safely to their waiting parents.

Thank You, Father God, that Jesus is our ark. He's the one who saves us and shelters us through the storms of life.

Erin took a deep breath to relieve the sudden pressure in her chest and headed for the sanctuary. She'd been waiting and praying seven years for Alayne to come back to the Lord. How long would she have to wait for that storm to be over?

The sound of organ music penetrated her thoughts. Erin pushed on the swinging door, slipped through the slight opening, then slid into a pew and reached for a hymnal. *Lord, please draw Alayne back to You. I ask it in Your holy name. Amen.*

The first selection was "Amazing Grace." Erin smiled at its appropriateness, slipped the hymnal back into the rack and sang the words straight from her heart.

■ ■ ■ ■

He hated Sunday mornings! Everyone slept in to get over Saturday nights. There was nothing going on — nothing to distract him.

Erin was probably in church.

David frowned. He needed to get over this attraction for Erin. He'd been making some progress at that until he ran into her at the store. And then that game in the park! That had given him a serious setback. Still, he knew what he wanted, where he was going and what he had to do to get there. And he was right on track. He wasn't about to stop now. Not even for Erin Kelly.

David raked his hands through his hair, flopped down on the couch and propped his feet up on his ebony coffee table. Boy, that woman was messing with his head — with his *life!* Brandee was in a snit because of last night. Not that he blamed her. Charlene's parties were important to people trying to scale the social ladder, and he might as well have stayed home for all the attention he paid everyone. Especially Brandee.

David winced and clasped his hands behind his head. He'd really missed the ball on that one! Brandee had even told him in

70

advance she'd bought a new dress and he ignored it. Well, that wasn't exactly true, but his compliment was tepid at best. The expensive, "barely there" dress that left little to the imagination had left him cold. He couldn't very well tell her that!

David frowned and snapped forward to a sitting position. That certainly wasn't the case with Erin Friday night. She was so appealing, even in her jeans and sleeveless sweater, it was a struggle to keep from taking her into his arms. And when he'd tried to warm her —

David leaped to his feet and shook his head. He didn't want to think about the emotions that rushed through him at that moment. Suffice to say, he hadn't been prepared for the force of them. He gave a short bark of a laugh. Hadn't been prepared? There was a master of understatement! He'd been rocked back on his heels for sure. And he was no novice in the romance department. He — "Arrrgh!"

David strode to his desk, grabbed the portable phone off the base and punched a button.

"Hey! Ted Burton speaking. I can't answer right now, so leave a message. If it sounds interesting, I'll give you a call back." There was a beep.

David slapped the handset onto the base, spun on his heel and headed for his bedroom. He'd go down to the fitness center and find someone he could challenge to a good, hard game of handball. That would drive Erin Kelly out of his mind!

"I've never been on public assistance in my life and I don't want to start now. I take care of my own! It's just that — since the plant laid a bunch of us off — I haven't been able to find work, and what I had set aside is almost gone. My unemployment insurance isn't enough to cover everything."

Erin's heart swelled with compassion as the young woman sitting across from her knitted her work-roughened hands together on the desk.

"The truth is —" Shame stole the proud lift of the woman's head and slumped her shoulders as the knuckles on her hands whitened with tension. "I can't read or write well enough to fill out the application forms when I go apply for a job." The woman lifted her head. Fierce pride shone in her blue eyes. "I'm a good worker! And I learn fast. If they'd just let me *tell* them what I can do . . ."

It was an all-too-familiar lament. "I understand, Ms. Wallace. And, believe me, you're not alone." Erin kept her tone businesslike and respectful, without any hint of what might be perceived as pity.

"I'm not?"

There was relief in Janet Wallace's voice. Erin gave her a warm smile. "Not at all. We see many people with similar difficulties."

"Really?"

The starch went out of the potential student's spine. Erin gave her another smile. "We certainly do. And we're able to help them all."

"How long does it take?" Worry clouded the young woman's blue eyes. "Like I said, what I had set aside is almost gone, and I have a little girl. . . ."

"There's no set answer to your question, Ms. — May I call you Janet?" The young woman nodded. "The length of time needed will depend on your ability, your goals and how hard you're willing to work to achieve them. Let me ask you some questions that will help me determine those things and we'll take it from there."

Erin pulled her keyboard forward. "I'll need a little background information first. Where did you go to school?"

"East End High."

"Did you graduate?"

"Yeah, for all the good it did me."

"Hey, Dave." Homicide detective Don Gallo rose to his feet and stuck out his hand. "Thanks for making time to come in." He grinned. "Not that you reporters actually work for a living."

David returned the grin and shook hands. "Better be nice, Don, you need me. I hear the other witness folded on you."

The detective's grin faded. "Yeah. He backed off when he got a threatening phone call." He gave him a sharp look. "You should have reported yours."

David shrugged. "I didn't take it seriously. The guy said he saw me on TV. I figured he was getting his kicks trying to play mind games with me."

"Well, if it happens again, report it immediately."

"Oh?" David's reporter radar went on alert. "Why? What's involved here? Drugs? A turf war? Or — ?"

"No." The detective led the way down a cheerless corridor. "Near as we can determine, this was strictly a personal vendetta. The victim was playing games with the suspect's girl." He reached for the knob on a closed door.

David frowned. "And?"

Don Gallo looked over his shoulder at him. "And what?"

"And that's not enough to explain why you're warning me about the possibility of another threat when this guy will be behind bars. What's the rest of the story?"

The detective shook his head and twisted the knob. David turned and started back the way they had come.

"What the — ? Get back here, Carlson!" There was the sound of footsteps slapping against the tile floor as Don Gallo hurried to catch up to him. "Where do you think you're going? The lineup room is that way." The detective jerked his thumb the other direction.

"I've changed my mind about testifying. I'm going for coffee." David looked full into Don Gallo's irritated gaze and smiled. "Care to join me?"

The detective's jaw worked back and forth. He looked up and down the hall. "All right, what do you want to know?"

"For starters, what took so long? I thought you'd call me to ID the shooter right away."

"Investigations take time."

David waited.

"All right, he went underground. Took us a while to find him."

"I see." David studied Don Gallo's scowling face for a moment, then nodded. "Okay. I'll accept that edited version for now. But, I expect the details when you're able to tell them *and* an exclusive on this story."

"You — !"

"Uh-uh." David wagged his finger in the air. "Be nice, Gallo. Remember, you need me." He folded his arms and leaned one shoulder against the wall as if he had all the time in the world.

The detective gave a curt nod. "All right, you've got it."

"There, see how easy that was?" David smiled and straightened. "One more thing. If he went underground, he has to have connections. Who is this guy?"

Don Gallo shook his head.

David grinned and rested back against the wall.

The detective's face tightened. "All right, you win, Carlson. But it'll compromise the bust if I tell you now. I'll tell you after you ID him."

David straightened. "Deal. Let's go."

The detective nodded and led the way to the room. There were two men waiting inside — expensively dressed lawyer types. When they looked his way, David recognized Brian Sturgis, an assistant district attorney, and Frank Calabria, a lawyer with strong ties to the underground. He shot a look at Don Gallo.

The detective ignored him — and everyone else in the room — stepped to the side of a large one-way window and keyed an intercom. "Send 'em in."

Gallo glanced his way as a line of men entered the other room and faced the window. "Take your time. I want you to be sure."

David nodded.

The detective keyed the intercom again. "Have 'em turn."

David watched as the five men on the other side of the window turned right, paused, turned left, paused, then faced forward again.

"Need anything else? Want 'em to turn again?"

David shook his head.

Don Gallo frowned. "So do you recognize anyone?" He gestured toward the line of men. "Is the guy you saw shoot the victim there?"

Frank Calabria fastened a hard look on him. Brian Sturgis stepped between them to block it. David ignored them both. "Yes. The shooter is number four."

"You're sure?"

"I'm positive."

The stiffness left Gallo's body. He turned and punched the intercom, again. "That's all. Take 'em out."

Brian Sturgis stepped forward. "Thank you. You've been a big help." David nodded. The assistant D.A. opened the door and waved for Calabria to precede him into the hallway. The lawyer gave David another long look, then stepped to the door. David started after him. Maybe he'd get a story out of —

"Wait!"

David stopped. Don Gallo pulled out a pen, scribbled something into a small notebook then ripped off the page and handed it to him. "You can reach me at that number anytime day or night. If you get another threat, call me."

David frowned and tucked the paper in his pocket. "Another threat? I've already identified this guy."

Don Gallo shrugged, glanced down the hall at the departing lawyers and lowered his voice. "We still have to get an indictment and a conviction. It wouldn't be the first time a witness has been warned off from testifying in front of the grand jury or at a trial."

David reached out and pulled the door

closed. "Okay, Gallo. You can stop tap-dancing around the issue, I get the message. This guy is tied to the mob. Who is he?"

Gallo shot a glance toward the closed door. "The perp's name is Benny Vida. He's Angelo Vida's brother."

David let out a long, low whistle.

"Remember, you didn't hear it from me. And you can't write the story yet — it'll ruin our case." The detective gave him a measuring look. "You gonna bail out on us now?"

David shook his head. "You know me better than that, Gallo."

"Yeah, I know you." The detective stepped closer, put his hand on the knob of the door. "Look, Carlson, like I said earlier, this was a personal vendetta, not a hit. It doesn't involve the mob. But you don't want to mess with Angelo Vida. That's another reason not to write the story now. It will tie you in even closer." He jerked his head toward the door. "Not that that dirtbag won't tell Angelo who you are. That hand-some mug of yours is on the TV too often for him not to have recognized you. And the assistant district attorney will have to tell him anyway. Disclosure!" He snorted. "Calabria will try all the legal mumbo jumbo first, but if that fails — Well . . . you need to be careful."

David nodded. "I'll be careful, I'm no hero, Gallo. But I won't be scared off either. I've never seen a man murdered before. I want you to nail this guy." He opened the door and stepped out into the hall. "And don't worry, I'll hold the story until you say I can print it."

The echo of his footsteps followed him down the hall as he walked away.

CHAPTER SIX

"This was so good, Mom! And there's enough left for Dad when he gets home." Erin snapped the top on the plastic storage container and put it in the refrigerator. "No matter how I try, I can't make my lasagna taste like yours. I miss your cooking."

"It's been a while." Her mother poured the extra tomato sauce into another container and handed it to her. "I miss *you*."

"What? Only me? Not my culinary efforts?" Erin grinned and set the sauce in the fridge by the lasagna.

Her mother laughed. "You've a ways to go in the cooking department, my dear."

"Why, Mom, I'm shocked!" Erin fell back against the closed refrigerator door and clasped her hands over her heart. "How can you *say* such a thing to me?"

"Because it's true, Miss *Barrymore*." Her mother grinned and picked up the empty sauce pan. "Now stop emoting and put away those place mats while I load these dishes. When I'm finished we'll go look at the garden. The new tree peony I put in is beautiful!"

"You sure have a green thumb, Mom." Erin swept her gaze over the riot of blooms around her. "The garden is so lush!"

"Thank you, dear. I enjoy working in it. And speaking of working, do you like being at the center full time?"

Erin pulled her nose away from the rose she was sniffing and nodded. "I really do." She gave a rueful smile. "I'll never get rich working there, but I like helping people. And teaching our clients to read and write really improves their lifestyle. It's wonderful to see their excitement when they get a better job because they can fill out an application, or earn a promotion because they're able to take a test."

"That must be rewarding. I'm proud of you, Erin." Her mother gave her a quick hug. "Success isn't always about making money."

"I know, Mom. But sometimes it feels like it." She grimaced. "For instance, now, when my car insurance is due."

"Erin! You *know* —"

"I'm *not* taking money from you and Dad,

Mom. I have enough. It just makes me skate a little close to the edge for a couple of weeks." Erin gave her a cheeky smile. "Besides, it's good for my character. Builds humility and self-discipline. You wouldn't want to rob me of those blessings, would you?" She ducked her head and looked up at her mother from under her lashes, the way she'd done when she was little. "Would you?"

Her mother's lips twitched with her effort not to smile. "Erin Teresa Kelly, you're not fighting fair!"

"I know. Guess who I learned that little tactic from?" Erin laughed and kissed her mother on the cheek. "I'm fighting honest, Mom, and you know it."

"Yes, I do." Her mother sighed and raked her fingers through her curly cap of dark hair. "All right, Erin. I won't insist. But if —"

"I know you're here, Mom. And if things start to pinch, I'll squeal for you and Dad. I promise. Now —" she turned and started walking along the slate walk "— where is that tree peony you wanted to show me?"

"Over by the fountain."

Erin turned to her left. "Oh, wow, that *is* pretty!" She reached out and touched the flower. "These blossoms are *huge!*"

"Aren't they?" Her mother stepped up beside her. "I just love them — they're such a rich creamy color. And speaking of being rich —"

"Mom! I'm not taking your money!"

"Just kidding, honey." Her mother laughed and turned toward the house. "Let's go sit on the porch and have a glass of iced tea. You can tell me about this reporter you're dating."

"Reporter I'm dating? Who told — ? Alayne!" Erin hurried to catch up with her mother. "Did Alayne come home?" She couldn't quite mask the hope in her voice.

"No, dear. But she did call — and that's something to be thankful for — even if it was only because she needed me to send her a copy of her birth certificate." Her mother took a deep breath and squared her shoulders. "At least she talked with me for a few minutes. It was a blessing to hear her voice. Now . . . let's have that tea. And you can tell me all about the reporter." Her brow creased into a frown. "What was his name? Carter? No . . ." She pushed open the screen door and stepped inside.

"It's Carlson. David Carlson." Erin grabbed the screen door before it could close and hurried after her mother. "And I'm sorry to disappoint you again, Mom, but I'm not dating him." She softened her voice trying to take away the sting of her words. "You know better than that."

Her mother turned and looked at her. "Yes, I know. But I keep hoping and praying." She heaved a sigh, and pulled the pitcher of tea from the refrigerator. "Maybe you should give counseling another try, Erin. Your father and I will gladly pay for it. You have to get over this distrust of men before it destroys your chance for a normal life!"

"I know, Mom —" Erin draped her arm around her mother's shoulders and gave her a hug "— I'm trying."

Her mother reached up and patted her hand, then stepped out from under her arm and went to the cupboard for glasses. "No one can ask for more, honey. Just don't be discouraged, Erin. I'll continue to pray. God will show the way."

Erin parked in the garage, kicked her shoes off just inside the connecting door to her kitchen and walked straight to her piano in the living room. The smooth, cool feel of the keys against her fingertips released the coil of tension in her stomach. She closed her eyes and let her fingers have their way, listening as the tune of a favorite hymn filled the room.

Tears stung the backs of her eyes. How many hours had she logged on the piano playing away her disappointment and praying for her family? Especially Alayne. When would her sister change her rebellious ways?

Erin broke off the thought and stared down at the keyboard, her attention caught by the simple chorus she was playing. She began to hum the melody her fingers picked out and suddenly words poured into her mind. She gave them voice.

"When the Spirit of the Lord touches my
    soul.
When I yield to Him and give Him full
    control;
Then my life begins to change and I am
    never again the same;
When the Spirit of the Lord touches my
    soul."

And there was her answer. Alayne would change when she again yielded her heart to the Lord. Oh, if only it would happen soon! Her mother and father were so sad. They tried to hide it, but she could see it in their eyes and hear it in their voice whenever Alayne was mentioned. And her own heart ached for her sister. And for herself.

Erin stopped playing and clenched the edge of the piano bench. She *hated* Mr. Gorseman!

Hated.

Guilt settled like a blanket over Erin's spirit. She sighed and closed her eyes. "I'm sorry, Lord. I know I'm supposed to forgive those who sin against me — and I try. But I confess I'm not there yet. Please help me, by Your grace, to get over the anger. And please take this distrust and fear that is ruining my life from me. And please, *please* soften Alayne's heart by Your touch and pour out Your grace upon her that she might yield to You.

"Your word is truth, Lord, and Your word says, 'Train up a child in the way he should go, and when he is old, he will not depart from it.' Our mother and father love You, Lord, and they trained us in Your ways. I'm standing with them and believing You to draw Alayne back to Your loving arms. Thank You for the comfort of Your word, Lord. I ask these things —" the phone rang "— in Your name. Amen."

Erin scooted off the piano bench and ran to pick up the receiver. It was probably her mother calling to make sure she made it home safely. Her mother's anxieties were *another* legacy from Mr. Gorseman.

"Hello?"

"Hi, Boots. Just wanted to call and let you know that Jerry and I are going away for the weekend. Maybe longer. It depends on how things go. I didn't want you to worry if you called and I didn't answer."

It depends on how things go. Erin frowned. She didn't like the sound of those words *or* of her sister's voice. "Thanks, Alayne, I would have worried." She decided to do a little judicious probing. "Is something special going on? About the trip, I mean? Is it for Jerry's job, or —"

"No. Nothing special. Just want to get away . . . together. He's been working so hard on this new sales campaign, I've hardly seen him lately. He's been traveling throughout the entire region and that involves staying away, sometimes a week or more at a time. You know how it is."

The image of Jerry locked in the passionate embrace with the receptionist flashed into her mind. *I do indeed, Alayne. Do you?* "Yes, I know." Erin curled up in a corner of the couch, groping for something to say that would keep Alayne talking while she listened for clues to this new problem, whatever or *whoever* it was. Her sister would never come right out and admit there was a problem in her relationship with Jerry. "Where are you going?"

"No place special. Just . . . away. Maybe we'll fly to Vegas. Jerry likes Vegas."

Jerry likes to gamble! And you hate it — though you'd never say so. "You'll melt, Alayne! It's hot out there this time of year."

"The casinos are air-conditioned." There was a quick indrawn breath. "Look, I've got to go, Erin. I want to be packed and ready to go if — I mean — *when* Jerry gets home tonight." There was a little, forced laugh. "I *told* you he's been away a lot lately. Don't expect me any specific time. I'll call when we get back. Bye."

"Bye, Alayne."

She knew. Erin stared off into space, her heart hurting for her sister. Alayne was so alone. When she'd turned her back on God, saying if God was so loving and powerful He should have protected Erin, the chasm her act created in the family was too wide for Alayne to cross — for any of them to cross — no matter how much they longed to heal the breach. Because of her lifestyle, Alayne couldn't face them. *Wouldn't* face them. She knew their Christian values.

Erin sighed and pushed to her feet. "Lord, I may be unable to trust a man, but I trust You. I have the peace and comfort of Your presence. Alayne doesn't. Have mercy on her, Jesus, and help her find her way home to You, I pray."

"I'll be back, Hank. Nick can't avoid me forever."

"Lemme give ya some advice, Carlson. Stop nosing around. Nobody's gonna talk to you."

"Just give Nick my message. I can't believe Vida has him running scared." David turned his back on the scowling bartender of the Three Circles Bar and Grill and stepped outside.

The cell phone in his inside jacket pocket vibrated. He pulled it out and hurried across the sidewalk to the edge of the street. "David Carlson."

"Hello, Carlson, Don Gallo."

"Hey, Gallo." David tightened his grip on the phone and sprinted across the road to the accompaniment of blaring horns. "What's up?"

"Sounds like a jaywalking bust to me." The homicide detective's voice growled into his ear. "Didn't your mama teach you to cross *with* the light?"

David grinned. "Details, *details,* Detective. You haven't done your homework. You should know my mama died when I was four years old."

"I *would* know it, along with the color of your toothbrush and which sock you put on first, if I was investigating you." There was an underlying note of tension in the light words. "Where are you?"

David snapped to attention. "Why?"

"Stop playing games, Carlson. Answer the question."

"I'm standing beside my car."

"Da —"

"Uh — uh, Detective, no swearing. Didn't *your* mama teach you that wasn't nice?" David grinned and yanked the phone away as a string of expletives exploded into his ear.

"Stop joking around, Carlson! *Where are you?*"

David heard the roar even holding the phone a foot away from his head. His grin faded. He pulled the phone back in place. "I'm on Charles Avenue. Why?"

"Charles — get in your car! *Now!*"

All friendliness had fled the detective's voice — he was pure business. David punched the lock/unlock button on his key ring, opened the door and slid behind the wheel. He wasn't feeling very friendly himself. "All right, Gallo, give!" He yanked his seat belt across his chest and snapped it into place. "Is this about Vida?"

"Yeah. Start driving. I want you out of that area."

David started the car, checked traffic and pulled away from the curb. "Okay, I'm driving."

"Come down to the station."

David made a right onto Lincoln Drive. "You have to do better than that, Gallo. I'm a busy man. I have a story to investigate and write."

"Look, Carlson, we've been picking up street talk that doesn't bode well for you. Get in here!"

"Anything specific, or just rumors?"

"Rumors, but with Angelo —"

"Thanks anyway, Gallo, but I'll take a pass. I'm not letting you lock me up in some hideaway because Angelo Vida is making threats."

"Carlson —"

"No." David glanced in his rearview mirror — the conversation was making him edgy. "The best way for you to protect me is to catch the bad guys. Meanwhile, I have a life to live and a job to do. I'm not independently wealthy and my landlord likes his rent on time."

"Yeah, I know the problem." The voice growling into his ear had lightened. David twisted his mouth into a wry grin. Evidently

Gallo had decided to go back to the friendly approach. "Look, Carlson, I can't force you to come in —"

"Which is why I'm not going to." David eased up on his attitude. The detective was only doing his job. "You wouldn't either if you were in my position."

"Well I sure wouldn't be sticking my head in the lion's den asking questions!" There was frustration in the deep, gravely voice. "Look, at least stay out of the west side; there's no sense in giving Angelo the advantage of home turf."

A chill slid down David's spine. He scowled. "I'll try, but if a story takes me there —"

"Let someone else do your legwork in that area till this case is over! You can't write a story if you're lying on a slab in the morgue."

The chill came again. David's scowl deepened. "Good point. I'll take it under consideration."

"You'd better do more than consider, Carlson. This is no joke. Angelo Vida doesn't play games — he plays for keeps."

Gallo sounded tired. Guilt smote David. "I know. I appreciate the warning. I'll be careful."

"One more thing. I'm going to assign

some black-and-whites to patrol the area around your apartment building until after the grand jury sits. Then, if Vida's indicted, we'll go from there. What we do will depend on the trial date."

"Any more good news?"

Gallo chuckled. "Nah, that's all." There was a pause. "I'll do what I can for you, Carlson, but I'm afraid it's not much. Watch your back, keep that cell phone handy and *stay out of the west side.*"

The phone went dead. David tossed it on the seat, then thought better of it, snatched it up and slid it in his pocket. He checked his mirrors again, flipped on his blinker and passed the large white van ahead of him. He was feeling boxed in and he didn't like it. He didn't like it at all.

If he could get his hands on Don Gallo . . . ! David paced the length of his living room, turned and paced back to circle the couch and started the lap over again. How was he supposed to find his big story now that the detective had made an end run around him and involved his boss!

Concentrate on your special features column, Dave — enlarge on it. We'll run it three times a week, or maybe make it a daily, but no more investigative reporting work until after

Vida's trial. That's an order! You're my star reporter, and I don't want to lose you.

David scowled, swung his arms through the air to relax the tension in his shoulders and stopped to stare out the window. A black-and-white patrol car crawled along the street below. Great! Just great! Maybe he could turn that into an article. He could title it The View From An Eyewitness's Window. He sure didn't have anything else!

David scrubbed his hand over the back of his neck, turned from the window and headed for his study. He probably should be grateful Gallo hadn't put him in protective custody. He could still go out and do what he wanted. He just couldn't go where the stories were.

Human interest stuff. David snorted and crossed to his desk. He'd never draw the attention of the TV news network moguls with that. He needed something big! Something important enough to make a stir and get people talking. Meanwhile he had . . . what? He opened the computer file of special-feature stories he'd done and started scanning the list. Maybe he could . . .

David stopped scrolling down the column, narrowed his eyes and peered at the words by the cursor: *Westwood Literacy Center Grant.* That might work. He let go of the mouse and picked up the phone.

Erin jumped at the strident ring of the phone, crossed to the desk and picked up the receiver. "Hello?"

"Hello, Erin. This is David Carlson."

David Carlson? Why was he calling? Erin sat on the couch and pulled a pillow onto her lap, her fingers playing with the cording around the outside of it as she mentally sorted through possibilities. "What a coincidence. I was going to call tomorrow to tell you how much Professor Stiles liked the article you wrote about the grant. He's very grateful for your accurate and respectful report — his words."

"Good. I'm glad he was pleased. And that brings me to the reason I'm calling. How was your day?"

Her day? "Satisfying . . . and heart rending." She hoped he couldn't hear her confusion in her voice. "A young woman came into the center today because — Well, the reason she came doesn't matter." Erin tossed the pillow aside and shoved off the couch. "David, she can't read, write or do anything but simple math. And she graduated from high school last year."

Erin walked to a front window, turned and stormed over to the antique secretary that graced the far wall. "It just makes me enraged that this is happening! Instead of hiring qualified, first-rate educators and aides to teach our children, schools are making the tests easier! And with all the federal and state aid they receive, why *can't* they buy books for students? One of my students told me he had to share his book with *three* other children. No wonder the center is being overwhelmed with clients!"

She caught a glimpse of her angry face in the window as she strode by and stopped pacing. "Sorry. I got carried away. But it just makes me *furious.* It's shameful! The education department is not doing its job and no one seems to care. At least not enough to bring it out in the open and find some answers." She paused for breath. There was silence on the other end of the line.

"David?" He chuckled. A low, soft chuckle that did queer things to the pit of her stomach. "Did I say something funny?"

"No. It's only that I've been racking my brain trying to come up with a big story, and I think you may have just handed it to me on a silver platter."

"I have?"

"You have. Listen, Erin, I called because I wanted to get together and talk with you about how things had changed since the grant money arrived. I was going to do a follow-up article about the center. Now, thanks to you, I have a better idea. Would you have dinner with me tomorrow night so we can discuss it?"

"I certainly would! This sounds interesting. And I don't work late at the center tomorrow." Erin plopped back down on the couch. "Do I get a hint as to what this idea is about?"

"Nope — not until tomorrow night. I want to check some things out before we talk about it. So, dinner tomorrow at the Bradbury Inn. How's seven o'clock?"

"Seven is fine."

"Okay, I'll pick you up at six-thirty."

"David, wait!" Too late. He'd already hung up. Erin stared down at the phone, conscious of her heart hammering against her ribs. She'd have to call him back. She jerked to her feet and went to get the phone book and look up his home number.

What excuse could she give for not riding with him? She'd already told him she didn't have to work. And she could hardly say, sorry, but I always take my own car because I'm afraid to be alone with a man! Erin nibbled at her lip trying to think of something honest and believable, but came up dry. She closed the phone book and put it back in the drawer. She was stuck. She'd just have to make the best of it, unless something came to her in the meantime.

Erin went back to the couch, sat in the corner and curled her legs beneath her. So she had given David an idea for a big story. What could it be? She crossed her arms over her chest and rested her chin on the handset cradled in her hands as she went back over their conversation. Obviously, it had something to do with the center, but what?

CHAPTER SEVEN

"You're doing great, Susan. You've learned how to write a check and enter it in the register, now we'll do a deposit." Erin pulled a copy of a deposit slip for a local bank out of a folder and placed it on the table in front of Susan Jansen.

"This is where your name and address will be printed." She indicated the bogus name and address on the phony deposit slip. And this —" she pointed to the line of zeros on the bottom of the slip "— is where your account number, the same account number that's on the bottom of your checks, will be printed. There will be other numbers there as well, but you needn't concern yourself with them; they're basically for the bank's information." She looked up at Susan. "Any questions?"

"No. I understand . . . so far."

Erin's heart squeezed at the rueful smile the young woman gave her. "You're doing fine, Susan."

"Yeah, now!" Anger flashed in the teenager's eyes. "I could learn this stuff in school if I had someone like you to help me. The classes are so crowded even the *good* teachers haven't time to help anyone that can't keep up. Students like me just sort of sit there until they pass us on because of our age, or the class size or something." She sighed. "Anyway, thanks to you, I don't feel like such a dummy now, and I'm catching up."

Erin smiled. "That's wonderful, Susan. It's why we're here. Now, let's get back to the deposit." Erin sent a silent thankful prayer heavenward as Janet Wallace — who had seemed so reluctant during her initial interview — came through the door and walked over to meet her tutor. Erin sighed her relief and pointed at the top box on the right side. "This is where you write in any cash deposit. The boxes beneath it are where you list any checks you want to deposit."

Susan frowned. "Why does this box say 'total from other side'?"

"There are more boxes on the back if you have a lot of checks to deposit. That line is for the subtotal. And this line —" she indicated the spot "— is for the overall total of the money and checks being deposited."

She looked up as Susan Jansen sighed. "Am I going too fast?"

"No. I was just thinking how neat it will be to get a good grade on the test we have coming up. Mr. Baker will sure be surprised. And you know what else?"

"What?"

The teenager grinned. "Monday I'm going to the bank and open a checking account. I've been doing everything with cash because I didn't understand this stuff."

Erin smiled her pleasure. "Then we'd better get to the next step." She picked up her pen. "You enter the deposit in the register in this column." She wrote in an amount. "Then, when you write a check, you take the amount of the balance on the line above . . . add the deposit to it . . . subtract the amount of the check . . . and enter the balance here."

Erin finished her demonstration and pushed the paper toward the girl. "Now you try it. Make up any amount you want for the deposit and check." She watched closely as Susan did as instructed. "Excellent! That's exactly right."

Susan beamed. "It's not hard to get the hang of it once it's explained. I just have trouble trying to learn it from a book on my own. Thanks, Ms. Kelly. When I come back next Monday, will you show me how to figure out a bank statement? That'll be on the test, too."

Erin smiled at her. "I certainly will. And not just because of the test. That bank statement is important. If you don't know how to reconcile it with your checkbook, you can get into big trouble." She gathered up the papers. "Would you like to keep these for reference?"

"Yeah. That's a good idea." Susan took the papers and headed for the door. "Thanks again. See you Monday."

"You're welcome." Erin returned the teenager's wave, then glanced at her watch. Only five minutes until closing time. She would soon be on her way home to get ready for dinner with David. It wouldn't be long until she found out what this big story idea involving the center was. She tamped down the wave of excitement at the thought and went to stand by the door to bid people goodnight during the general exodus of tutors and clients.

Erin studied her reflection while she made a slow turn. The creamy yellow color of the dress looked good with her dark-red hair, and the sloped cut of the bodice falling away from the thin neck band was flattering. She had nice shoulders. Didn't she? She scowled and leaned closer to the mirror. Maybe her shoulders were too bony. Maybe she should wear the green . . .

Erin's heart leaped into her throat as the doorbell rang. That couldn't be David already, could it? She shot a glance at her alarm clock. *Six-thirty!* Where had the time gone? She grabbed her white strap sandals from the closet and yanked one on. "That's what I get for being so nerved up that I couldn't make a decision! Now I'm stuck with bony shoulders showing and —" the bell rang again "— only one shoe on!"

Erin limped by the bed, then hobbled down the stairs to open the door. "Hello, David."

"Hi." His gaze met hers, then dropped to the sandal in her hand. "Looks like I'm a little early."

"Not at all. You're right on time." Erin braced her hand against the door frame and leaned down to tug her other shoe on. Her hair fell forward. She tucked it behind her ear and straightened. "There! Now I'm all together."

David's gaze swept over her, came to rest on her face. "You certainly are. And, may I say, you look beautiful."

He'd thought she was searching for a com-

pliment. Erin's cheeks heated. Could she have given him a more erroneous impression?

David smiled. "I like it when you blush."

The warmth in her cheeks increased several degrees. She took a breath. "Then you must be very pleased at the moment." It came out a tiny bit acerbic, which didn't help her blush at all.

David's smile widened. "I am."

Smooth. Very smooth. A nervous little quiver rippled through Erin's stomach. She grabbed her small white clutch bag off the table by the door and stepped out onto the porch, before she lost her courage and bolted back to her bedroom to change into something less attractive — like an old baggy sweat suit.

"You're not going to keep me waiting?" Shock spread across David's face. "You're ready to go?"

"I'm afraid so." *There was no way she would be alone with him in her house.* Erin closed the door and locked it. "There's no point in more primping. This is as good as it gets."

"It certainly is."

All right, Mr. Carlson, you can stop now. Erin's heart thudded as they moved down the steps side by side. The occasional brush of his arm against hers as they walked to his car didn't help matters. She concentrated on taking steady even breaths as David opened the car door and she slid inside. Her stomach knotted. She gripped her purse, her fingers seeking the reassurance of the small can of mace inside it as he shut the door and walked around the car to get in.

"Ummm."

"Ummm, what?" David flipped on his blinker and exited the highway in favor of Maple Grove Avenue.

Erin shook her head. "Nothing. I was just admiring the terra-cotta trim on that stucco house. It's my favorite color."

"Terra-cotta? There, now see that! You women complicate the simplest things." David gave her a phony scowl. "Colors are red, yellow, blue, orange, green and brown! And if we're doing the favorites thing, mine's blue."

Erin wrinkled her nose at him. She was having a good time. "*Simple* is right. What *color* blue is your favorite? Sky-blue, baby-blue, navy-blue, periwinkle-blue, marine-blue —"

"Okay, okay, I give up." David laughed and turned into the restaurant's tree-lined drive. "Let me get onto safer ground here.

What's your favorite food."

Erin grinned. "That depends. Is it summer or winter?"

David groaned and parked the car. "Okay, I asked for that. I take back my earlier comment about women complicating things. But you're dealing with a reporter here, lady. I know how to pin down an answer."

He unsnapped his seat belt and turned to face her. A cocky grin slanted his mouth. "You're at a fine restaurant on a beautiful autumn evening, and —" he glanced at his watch "— it's six-fifty."

She released the catch on her seatbelt and slid toward the door. "What's on the menu?"

David burst into laughter. "The way you wiggled out from under that, I guess it will be humble pie for me."

Erin grinned. "Would that be plain or à la mode?"

David growled, reached out and opened his door. "You should have been a reporter, Erin Kelly — you're relentless. I'm proud of you. Now, let's go eat."

Erin nodded. She was looking forward to dinner. David was turning out to be a lot of fun.

"I read your article in yesterday's paper

about the fire department, David. It was excellent, in my opinion. Factual, but sensitive." Erin laid down her fork and dabbed her mouth with her napkin. "Your interview with Fire Chief Watson was so real I felt as if I were right there talking to him myself."

She placed her napkin back on her lap and reached for her glass. "You made the chief's frustration with the politics that undermine his men's ability to do their jobs very clear. You're a wonderful writer." She took a swallow of water.

David cut off a bite of chicken and speared it with his fork. "I hope you really mean that, Erin, and aren't just stroking my ego."

His words startled her quiet. She stared across the table at him. Why would he think that of her? Was that the type of person he associated with?

He knows how to play the "climbing the social ladder to success" game with the best of them.

Erin frowned at the memory of Alayne's words. She'd been having such a good time she was forgetting herself. She set her glass down and looked at him. "Perhaps you're accustomed to dealing with that type of dishonest, self-serving person, David, but please don't class me with them. I'm a Christian — I don't lie. If I'd only wanted to say something complimentary to 'stroke your ego,' I'd have told you I like your tie, which, by the way, I do." She smiled at him to lighten the suddenly heavy atmosphere. "It has terra-cotta in it."

David glanced down. "So *that's* what terra-cotta is." He lifted his gaze back to meet hers. "I'm sorry, Erin. I didn't mean to sound as if I was questioning your motives or your honesty. I had a reason for asking if you really like the way I write."

"Oh? That sounds intriguing, and serious." Erin placed her napkin on the table beside her plate. "Is it connected to what you wanted to discuss this evening?"

"Definitely." David pushed his plate away and leaned forward. "Do you remember your comments about the education department?"

Conversation at the next table stopped. The man seated with his back to them shifted his position and turned his head slightly in their direction. *How rude!* Erin lowered her voice. "Yes, I remember. Is that your idea? To do a st—" She stopped, staring at the finger David had pressed to his lips.

"Are you finished with your meal, Erin?"

Had she said something wrong? "Yes, I'm finished."

109

"Then let's get out here." David motioned to their server, threw some bills on the table then shoved back his chair and escorted her from the room.

"This was a wonderful idea, David. I can't remember the last time I came out to the pavilion."

He gave her a contrite look. "It's the least I could do after rushing you out of the restaurant without giving you a chance to order dessert. But, when I recognized Superintendent Trent at the next table, I thought it was the wise thing to do."

Erin nodded. "Wise, indeed. My comments about his education department aren't very flattering." She watched David tuck his wallet into his pocket, then handed him his cone and took a lick of her ice cream. "Mmm, I love butter pecan!"

David grinned, stuck a couple of paper napkins into his shirt pocket then placed his hand on the small of her back and guided her through the crush of people under the striped canopy into the open. "Butter pecan is good, but it doesn't compare to double chocolate chunk." He took a bite out of the top scoop of his cone, chewed the piece of chocolate in it, then smacked his lips.

Erin laughed at his clowning. "To each

their own." She took another lick of her cone as they strolled toward the lake. Music from the pavilion mingled with the murmur of people's voices and flowed after them. They skirted around a volleyball game in progress.

"How are things going at the center?"

She glanced up at David and shook her head. "Busy and frustrating as ever. Part of my job is to interview new applicants, assess their needs then match them to the tutor I think is best able to help them. The problem is I'm running out of tutors. They're all volunteers, and most of them have only a couple of hours a week to give the center." She sighed. "I had three new applicants today and I had to add two of them to my own list. There isn't anyone else available to help them, and I can't tell them they'll just have to wait. They need help now."

"Hmm. We can't have that." He took a lick at his cone. "Do you advertise for volunteers?"

Erin shook her head. "The center doesn't have an advertising budget. We *do* post notices in the area — schools, libraries and churches — but, of course, after a time the posters are taken down and thrown away. And the ones at the schools result in more students, not more volunteers." Something cold fell on her hand. She glanced down. Her ice cream! She'd forgotten about it.

"You're dripping." David pulled a napkin from his pocket and held it out to her. "Better lick that thing." He took another bite out of his own cone.

Erin wiped the ice cream from her hand, then ran her tongue around the edge of her cone to catch all the other dribbles. "I appreciate your politeness, David, but my curiosity is getting the better of my good manners." She looked up at him. "When are you going to stop asking me about my work and tell me what you wanted to talk about?"

"That *is* what I wanted to talk about — at least in part." David took another lick of his cone. "You know, I'd forgotten how good an ice cream cone is."

"Not to mention messy." Erin wrinkled her nose at him. "You have ice cream on your chin."

He wiped it away. "Erin."

"Yes?"

"Please don't wrinkle your nose at me like that."

"What?" She gaped up at him. "I'm sorry, I don't — Why?" Her lungs went into a frozen state as David locked his gaze on hers.

"Because I respect you, Erin. And when you wrinkle your nose like that —" he took a breath and looked away "— well, just have a heart and don't do it, okay?" He lifted his cone to his mouth and took another lick. "Do you remember telling me about the deplorable state of our education system during our first meeting?"

Erin nodded. Did he really mean what he said about *respecting* her?

"Well, because of that, I was going to do a simple follow-up piece about the city's need for the center. That's why I called you last night, to set up a meeting. But, after talking with you on the phone, I spent the rest of the evening researching online. And today I've been calling some of my contacts and doing a little quiet probing."

David lowered his voice. "This is more than I expected. The ramifications of what I'm learning are *endless.* You've given me my big story, Erin. I'm going to do a series on the lack of quality education in our city, the reasons behind it and the effect it has on our community."

"David, that's wonderful!" Erin forgot about his statements — truthful or otherwise.

"I knew you'd think so." He took her arm, guided her away from a group of people sitting on the sand and headed down the beach. "I don't want this to be only a cut-and-dried piece of factual information, Erin." He stopped walking and faced her. "That will be part of it, of course, but I want to write the stories from the point of view of the people who are affected by the shortcomings in our education system. People like those who come to the literacy center. That way, the readers will understand that it's not simply a matter of dollars and cents, or even moral or legal right and wrong, but a matter of people's *lives*." He stopped pacing and looked down at her. "What do you think?"

"I think you're amazing." Erin's heart was pumping with excitement. "It's a fantastic way to reach the public with the truth!"

David fastened a sober gaze on her. "I'm glad you feel that way, because I'd like to interview some of your students. I'll protect their identities if they so choose, but I really need their stories to make this work. Will you help me convince them to talk with me, Erin? And help me get Professor Stiles on board?"

"Of course I will! But Professor Stiles will need no convincing, this is — I can't tell you —" Tears sprang to Erin's eyes. "It's wonderful, David."

He stared down at her. "Do you want that cone?"

Her heart thumped at the look in his eyes. She shook her head. "I've had enough."

"Wait here." David took her cone, walked over and tossed both their cones into a trash can, then came back and took hold of her hand. "Come on. Let's get away from this crowd where we can talk." He led her toward the stone jetty thrusting out into the lake a short distance away.

Erin stared down at their linked hands, aware of the warmth and strength of David's, wondering at the way hers felt so small encased in his. Why didn't she want to tug her hand out of his grip the way she always did with other men? Disappointment flickered through her when he let go. She focused on their conversation to stop her racing pulse. "You said you've done some research on the department of education. Are you looking at anything in particular?" He gave her a sidelong look that turned her effort at composure into a complete waste of time. What was happening to her?

"I've been studying the general picture — statistical comparisons with other school systems — that sort of thing. It seems our high school gives very high priority to its sports programs. Programs Superintendent Trent backs to full measure with the discretionary funds." David helped her onto the jetty then tightened his grip on her hand and moved over to walk along the edge of the concrete surface to give passing room to a departing fisherman carrying all his gear.

"But that's so unfair!" Erin frowned and stepped over a long, deep fissure in the cement. That money should be used to hire more teachers, or buy more supplies, or . . ." The squeeze of his hand broke her off. She glanced up at him and the look of admiration in his eyes started her pulse sprinting again.

"Slow down, Erin." David smiled and squeezed her hand again. "I knew you'd be incensed when I told you, but I have a lot more investigating to do before I know anything for certain."

She dragged her thoughts away from the havoc being raised in her stomach by his smile. "I know, I got carried away." She smoothed her hair back with her free hand. "Is that what you did today, study the school budget?" She smiled. "It must have been a dull day for you."

He shook his head and led her around a hole where one of the stones had given way.

"Not really dull — let's say quiet. I'm used to spending my days on the streets investigating leads. Like yesterday when I went to a bar to follow a lead about the murder suspect I identified for the police in a lineup. I —"

"You identified a *murder* suspect!" Erin came to an abrupt halt. David released her hand and turned to face her. She stared up at him. "Are you talking about the person who shot and killed that man on Humbard Street?"

David nodded. "That's the one."

"So you *did* see the shooting. I saw you on TV, standing in that doorway with another man and a police officer, but I hoped you were only covering the story for *The Herald.*" Erin's mind fastened on his earlier words. Her throat tightened. "He's a murderer!"

"*Alleged* murderer, until he's been found guilty."

Her breath caught in a little gasp. "You'll have to testify!"

He nodded.

Something cold slithered down her spine. Erin moved forward and stared down at the water lapping against the stones at the end of the jetty while every chilling scene of revenge from every murder mystery she'd ever read paraded across her mind. Fear for

117

David's safety twisted cold knots in her stomach. How many witnesses had been drowned in those stories?

"Forget about the killer, Erin. Let's talk about what you said." David stepped up behind her. "You said you *hoped* I wasn't a witness?"

His voice was quiet, thoughtful. Erin shivered and turned toward him, away from the water — it looked cold, dark and ugly in the fading twilight. "Yes, I did. It would be a horrible thing to see." She shuddered. "And, David, I know it really isn't any of my business, but isn't identifying that man *dangerous?* You were on TV. He'll know you're the one who identified him to the police. And that means he'll know you will testify in court."

David nodded. "That's true. But he'll also be in jail." He moved closer and fastened his gaze on hers. "Are you worried about me, Erin?"

Why else would her heart be pounding? "Well, of course I am." She tried to make her voice sound matter of fact, but it came out as a frightened whisper. She clenched her hands into fists and looked down at the front of David's shirt, fighting a sudden, unexplainable urge to throw herself into his arms. *She'd gone insane!*

118

"Erin?" The way he spoke her name made her swallow hard. She lost her breath as he placed the knuckle of his forefinger under her chin and lifted her head. "I like having you worry about me." His eyes darkened to the color of smoke and his hands left trails of heat as he slid them down her arms and clasped both her hands. "I like you." He tugged her closer.

Erin's pulse rocketed. She closed her eyes, reminding herself she must beware of this man and these strange new feelings he was rousing in her. She stepped back and took a deep breath. "I like you, too, David." She made her voice steady. Refused to let the sudden trembling inside her surface. "It will make working with you on your story a pleasure."

David pulled his car into her driveway and killed the motor. Erin's heart stuttered out erratic beats as he got out and walked around the car to open her door. She released her seat belt and pulled her keys from her purse.

"I'll take those."

Before she could object, David took the keys, helped her from the car and closed the door. His hand closed around hers as they walked to her porch. It felt right —

amazingly, wonderfully right. And so different from anything she'd ever experienced. The whole evening had been an assault on her senses and emotions.

Erin took a deep breath of the warm autumn night air and smiled up at David when they reached her door. "Thank you for dinner, David. And for the ice cream. I had a lovely time. And I'm really excited about working with you." She tried for a light touch to disguise her confusion. "Do I get a byline?"

David grinned. "No. You only get a byline if you do the writing. But I will give you credit and at least a dozen honorable mentions. I promise."

She smiled. "That's not necessary."

David studied her face, read the honesty in her eyes and shook his head. "You're a rare individual, Erin Kelly. Most people want all the credit and fame they can get." He dragged his gaze away from her mouth to squelch temptation. Somehow he didn't think she would appreciate it if he kissed her. There had been a moment — earlier when they were on the jetty — but not now. Something had made Erin draw back. Or maybe he'd simply misread her enthusiasm for his work as attraction for him. He turned and unlocked her door, then handed her the keys. "Good night, Erin."

He clenched his hands as she reached up and brushed a stray wisp of hair off her face. "Good night, David."

He opened her door and stepped back. She started inside. "Oh, I wanted to tell you —" she turned back "— I'm not positive because Professor Stiles keeps his own version of a schedule, but he may be at the center tomorrow. If so, I'll try and set up a meeting between you two. Would next Monday be convenient?"

"You set it up — I'll be there."

"All right, I'll call and let you —"

David shook his head. "I never know where I'm going to be, or what I'll be doing. I'll call you tomorrow night. We have a lot more to talk about."

"I'll look forward to it." She held out her hand. "Until tomorrow night, then."

He'd been right about the kiss. David took Erin's hand in his. Hers was trembling slightly. It had the effect of an electric shock on him. He forced a smile. "Until tomorrow." He watched as she went inside, then turned and walked away before he charged through the door, took her in his arms and kissed her until he was senseless.

The way he felt about her, it wouldn't take long.

The light was blinking. David tossed his suit jacket over the back of the couch and pushed the button on his answering machine.

"David, darling, where are you? It's been forever. Are you busy? Or dating someone? I know we date for convenience or professional need and that we're free to see other people, but I'm feeling neglected. You don't want me to feel neglected, do you?"

Brandee's voice grated on his ears. David scowled and tugged off his tie. How had he ever found that phony, pouty tone attractive? And that coy stuff! Erin never acted like that.

"Call me, darling. I have wonderful news. I've been chosen to do a swimsuit shoot in Hawaii and I get to take a friend along — all expenses paid. I choose you. And, as an added enticement, if the thought of me in a bikini isn't enough to make you want to come along —" There was a throaty laugh.

David's scowl deepened. Brandee's laugh was fake, too. He should know — he'd helped her perfect it. He shook his head and undid his collar button. There wasn't much about Brandee that was real. Erin on the

122

other hand — he paused with his fingers on the next shirt button — Erin was as real as they came.

"The magazine is hosting several parties through the week and having a *huge* bash at the end of the shoot. There will be oodles of influential people attending. And you know what that can mean for our careers if we play our cards right."

I'm a Christian — I don't lie.

Erin's words echoed through his mind. David rubbed at the nape of his neck, feeling underhanded and tacky at the thought of all the times he'd said something untrue just to schmooze someone who might help him advance his career as a journalist.

"David, darling, this could be *the* big break for both of us. You *must* come. Your dark good looks are the perfect foil for my fair beauty. We look so fabulous together I guarantee our picture will be all over the tabloids *and* in reputable magazines. And you know as well as I, a little notoriety works wonders to boost popularity with the public. And *that,* in turn, gains the notice of the right people."

David focused his attention. Brandee's voice had taken on that sharp edge it always had when she was calculating career moves.

"Maybe it's time we stop seeing other

people and concentrate on each other, David. Of course, once you see me in the bikini I'm wearing for the shoot, you might have trouble concentrating at all." Brandee's tone softened again. "We leave on the eighteenth and will return the twenty-fourth. Take some vacation time and come with me, David. You won't regret it — I promise. Ta, ta, darling. I'll be waiting for your call."

Her words faded away. David stood staring at the answering machine, trying to understand the feelings coursing through him — the thoughts chasing each other around in his head. He should feel pleased, *excited,* at the prospect of spending time with people who could advance his career. He should be crowing like a rooster at Brandee's invitation for an intimate week together. But all he felt was . . . disgust. And all he could think of was the difference between Brandee and Erin.

David punched the erase button, picked up his jacket and walked to his bedroom. He didn't want to probe into his emotions. It scared him to think of what he might find. But there was no denying that his perception on some things had changed since he'd met Erin Kelly.

He shot a look at his alarm clock. Too late to call Brandee tonight. Tomorrow morning he'd call and make a date for lunch. What he had to say should be said in person. Their mutual agreement was over. He wouldn't be escorting her to any more parties — in Hawaii, or anywhere else. He didn't want to be with any woman but Erin.

David stopped cold in his tracks, his heart thudding as the truth hit him. *He was falling in love with her!* The knowledge leaped from his heart to his head, searing itself into his consciousness.

He threw his jacket and tie into a chair and sank down on the edge of his bed, blown away by the truth. He was falling in love with Erin Kelly. The question was, what was he going to do about it?

CHAPTER EIGHT

Erin towel-dried her hair, tugged on her bathrobe then hummed her way into her bedroom. A bird, perched on the leafy limb outside her open window, chirped its pleasure in the day. Sunshine streamed in through the screen. She moved over to warm her bare feet in the golden pool it formed on the floor, and the bird spread its wings and flew away. She watched until it became a tiny speck in the distance. "Lord, I'm not able to fly — You didn't give me wings. But my heart is soaring to You this morning. I don't know what You did last night, but I thank You. I started on that dinner meeting with David full of the same old distrust and fear, and somehow I came home without it. You've lifted it from me, Lord, and I feel as free as that little bird. Thank You for the beautiful gift of freedom and for loving me."

Erin stood a moment longer, soaking in

the sunshine, then went to get ready for work.

"So how did Brandee take your news?"

David glanced at Ted and shrugged. "Not bad. She was a little ticked at the timing. She has this huge shoot in Hawaii coming up that grabs lots of media attention and she was planning to take advantage of that. She wanted to make a big romantic splash for the tabloids with me as her partner because I'm so all-fired good-looking." He grinned and struck a pose.

Ted groaned. "Modest, too."

"Yeah. That's another of my outstanding qualities." David laughed and picked up a chicken wing to dunk in the blue-cheese dip.

Ted finished his wing and took a swallow of soda. "Well, I can't say I'll miss Brandee — I never pretended she was my favorite person. Still . . . I'm curious. What made you give up your mutually beneficial admiration society?"

David shrugged. "I don't know. The admiration waned. And lately —" he frowned and wiped his fingers on his napkin "— lately, the benefits don't seem worth the price in self-esteem."

Ted paused with a steak fry halfway to his

mouth. "Run that by me again."

"You heard me."

"Yeah. But I'm not sure I understood you." Ted gave him his piercing "lawyer's look." "You always said having Brandee on your arm was good for your career. Why the change of heart?" He bit off half the fry.

David ignored the question and reached for another wing.

"Oh-ho! Wait a minute, buddy. I think I get it." Ted leaned against the back of the booth and locked his gaze on him. "It's that new religious woman you told me about — Erin. Yeah, that's it, isn't it?" His face split in a wide grin. "You've *fallen* for her. *That's* why Brandee has lost her appeal. And it explains that 'benefits not worth the price in self-esteem' remark. Erin's values are rubbing off on you."

David scowled. "Don't get carried away, Ted. You know how I feel about religion."

"Yes I do. That's what makes your attraction to this woman so surprising. Then again . . . when it's right, it's right."

"Knock it off."

Ted grinned and popped the other half of the steak fry in his mouth.

David threw down his chicken wing. "These things taste like cardboard today."

Ted laughed and reached for his soda.

"They taste fine to me. I'm over that first 'unable to eat' stage of love. I'm into the 'give me more food so I can keep up my energy' phase." He took a drink and picked up another wing. "So what are you going to do about it? The religious stuff, I mean."

David shoved his plate away and leaned back against the bench. "I don't know. I've been asking myself that same question. I guess I'm hoping, since Erin hasn't tried to force her beliefs onto me so far, things will work themselves out. What do you think?"

"I think that's 'pie in the sky,' pal." Ted shook his head. "I don't envy you, Tiger. This is one problem I wouldn't want to have to deal with. And I'm afraid I've no words of wisdom to offer you. I'm just a happy-go-lucky heathen, who plans on staying that way." He motioned to David's abandoned plate. "If you're not going to finish those wings, pass that blue-cheese dip over here. Mine's all gone."

"Perfect." Robert Stiles slapped his palm down on his desk. "Perfect!"

Erin glanced over at David. How could he be so calm?

"Then you agree, sir?"

Professor Stiles tipped his head down and looked at David over top of his glasses. "Do

I look like a fool to you, young man? Of course I agree! I've been trying to get the problems in our schools recognized by the public for years! This will do it." He leaned back in his chair. "There is a condition to the center's involvement, however."

David sat up a little straighter. "And that is?"

"Erin sits in on every interview. In this day and age of frivolous lawsuits, I don't want any possible hint of impropriety associated with the center *or* the story." The professor leveled another look on David. "I'm sure you don't either."

David nodded. "You're absolutely right. I was going to suggest Erin sit in on the interviews for that very reason. And also because I'm sure her presence will make your clients more relaxed and more likely to talk candidly with me."

"Yes, that's true." Professor Stiles nodded and rose to his feet. "If that's all, I have a plane to catch."

"Professor —" Erin rose and blocked his way to the door. "I want to clean out that small storage room at the end of the hall to use for the interviews. That way any clients who don't want to be seen talking with Da — Mr. Carlson, could come and go by the back door. It would afford them more privacy. But, I'll need a table and chairs." She smiled and indicated the furniture buried under stacks of old magazines and newspapers in the corner. "If I stack your papers neatly on the floor, for the time being, may I borrow those chairs?"

The professor glanced at the heavily laden chairs and scowled. "Very well. But don't lose any of my things." He gave her a fond look. "Using the back room is a good idea, Erin. Set it up any way you like. Now, if you'll excuse me, I'll be on my way. I'll see you next week, when I return from my speaking engagements."

David sprang to his feet. "Thank you, sir, for your cooperation. I promise you won't regret it."

"I'd better not, young man. I'm a formidable foe!" The professor shook David's offered hand and strode from the room.

David looked at her. Erin smiled so wide she thought her face would break. He stepped close and took hold of her hands. "You did it, Erin."

"No, David. It's your idea and he loved it. I can't wait to get started." She grinned up at him. "I'm going to pick out paint on my lunch hour and start cleaning out the back storage room after we close tonight. It

131

shouldn't take me more than a few nights to —"

David shook his head. "Us." He squeezed her hands. "Look, Erin, I have to go. I have an interview with Principal Pierce at three. But I'll be back tonight to help you clean and paint. It's the least I can do." Before she realized his intent, he tugged her into his arms and gave her a quick hug. "Thank you." He released her and stepped back.

"You're welcome." Erin stared after David, aware of the lingering feel of his arms around her as he walked away. He'd hugged her! And there was no nausea rising into her throat or uncontrollable shivering. Only a little trembling, and a fluttering in her pulse. The fear she would usually have at such an encounter truly was gone!

Erin shook her head to snap herself out of her bemused state and headed for her office. Two new clients were coming to see her this afternoon, and she had to find tutors for them.

She frowned and opened her office door as her mind shifted gears. Her problem was that every tutor's schedule was already filled to overflowing, including her own. Maybe David's articles would generate more volunteers to help at the center. But there was still the meantime.

Erin sighed and pulled up the scheduling file on her computer. There had to be someone. . . .

CHAPTER NINE

"The little girl hugged her mother and sat on the bench to put on her new red shoes. The end."

"Beth, that's wonderful!" Erin reached across the table and squeezed the beaming woman's hand. "You read the whole book and I didn't help you at all!"

"I know! Do I get to choose a new book now?"

"Absolutely!" Erin straightened and smiled at her. "We have several I think you'll —"

"I choose this one."

Erin looked down at the book the young woman pulled from a bag on the floor beside her chair. "A romance novel?"

Beth's lips split in a wide smile. "I've always wanted to read these books." Her smile faded. "Do you think I can?"

"Absolutely." Erin walked to the bookshelf on the side wall, pulled down a paperback dictionary, and returned to hand it to her pupil. "You may find a few words in the book you don't understand, but you can look them up in this dictionary. Do you know how to use it?" She tapped the romance book when Beth shook her head. "Pick out a word."

Beth opened the book. *"Trample."*

"All right. Now, the words in the dictionary are listed according to the alphabet." Erin handed her the book. "Find the words that begin with the letter *t.*"

She waited until Beth found the right place. "Now you look for the next letter in the word, *r.*" She nodded approval when Beth found it. "Now add the next letter, *a.*"

The young woman's eyes shone with excitement as she found the right spot. "Now, the *m?*"

"Yes." Erin waited.

"Trample! There's the word."

Erin nodded. "Now read what the dictionary says the word *trample* means."

"To tread underfoot. To crush with the feet. This is great!" Beth's eyes sparkled. "I can look up any word I don't understand, now. Thank you!"

"You're welcome, Beth." Erin followed her to the door, then walked down the hall to her office to change into her old jeans and a sweatshirt. Beth was her final appointment for the day and everyone else was gone. Now she could start cleaning out the back storage room.

Erin tugged a pile of old magazines and newspapers off a shelf into her arms. Dust rose into the air around her. She sneezed, sniffed and sneezed again.

"Gesundheit!"

The load in her arms crashed to the floor. She whirled toward the open door.

"Sorry." David stepped forward, knelt down and started gathering up the magazines and papers she'd dropped. "Why are you so startled? I told you I was coming to help."

"Yes, you did." Erin knelt down beside him. "I guess I was lost in thought. I didn't hear you come in."

He glanced up and that slow grin she was beginning to love spread across his face. "You have a smudge." He brushed his thumb over her cheek. "There, it's gone."

"Thank you." Her face tingled from the momentary contact. She grabbed a handful of the old newspapers and stood to put them in a box.

"Always happy to be of service." David threw her a smile, picked up the last of the magazines and rose. "What were you thinking about? My story? Me?" He brought his armful over to the table.

Erin shook her head. "As a matter of fact, no. I was thinking about decorating this room when it's painted."

David stared at her for a moment, then burst out laughing. "Erin Kelly, do you realize that you have this sassy side to your personality that rears its head every once in a while and puts me firmly in my place."

"And where would that be?"

His gaze captured hers. He dumped the magazines in a box and stepped around the corner of the table. "I'm not sure. But I hope it's —"

"Hey! Anybody here?"

Erin spun toward the door and almost fell. Her legs were trembling. She grabbed hold of the table for support.

"Down the hall on your left, Ted!" David glanced down at her hand clutching the table, then lifted his gaze back to fasten on hers. "We'll finish this conversation another time." He stepped back. "I told a friend of mine what we were doing, and he said if his fiancée was free, they'd come help us clean and paint the room. I hope —"

"Okay, we're here! What do we do, Dave?"

Erin jerked her head around toward the

door. A young man and woman stood there. She let go of the table and ran her fingers through her hair, hoping she didn't look as unstrung as she felt.

"Erin, this is Ted Burton and Darlene Collins." David nodded in the direction of his friends. "Darlene . . . Ted . . . this is Erin Kelly."

Erin smiled. "Hi. It's nice to meet you. Thanks for coming to help. It's very kind of you."

"No problem." Ted stepped into the room and looked around. "Where do we start?"

Erin waved her arm in an arc that encompassed the entire room. "Just grab hold of something and stuff it into one of those empty boxes —" she pointed toward a pile of cardboard containers in the corner "— then carry it down to the basement. I'll sort through everything later."

"Sounds easy enough." Ted grabbed a box and handed it to Darlene. "You load, I'll carry." He thumped David on the shoulder. "And *you* can buy the pizza later. I expect to work up a huge appetite."

David grinned. "So what's new?"

"The manual labor part." Ted twisted his face into a comical grimace. "We'll probably both feel this tomorrow. Neither one of us lifts anything heavier than a briefcase anymore." He picked up an already filled box off the folding table in the center of the room and turned to Erin. "Okay, let's get this show on the road! Show me the way to the basement."

"Many hands make light work. That's the last of the cleaning." Erin gave a final swipe to the dingy wood framing the window and tossed the rag in the bucket. "Now for the fun part. David, will you bring in the paint?"

There was a loud groan.

Erin turned around and grinned at Ted, who was sitting on the floor, leaning his back against the wall. He was so friendly she felt as if she'd known him for years. "Would you like to be excused from further participation in this event, sir?"

Ted shook his head. "Not on your life! I've come this far and I'm not stopping till I get that pizza. I'm a lawyer, I know my rights." He grinned and mimed struggling to his feet. "Just tell me what you want me to do next."

"Paint, buddy, paint!" David came back into the room holding a gallon pail in each hand. "I'll give you first choice. Which do you want to paint, ceiling or walls? Erin and Darlene are doing the trim."

"Walls."

David furrowed his forehead in a fierce scowl. "You're *supposed* to say ceiling. What kind of friend are you, taking the easy part?"

Ted grinned and shrugged his shoulders. "Hey, it's your story."

"So it is, thanks to Erin." David gave her a smile that brought warmth stealing into her heart. "And well worth the cost — I'll happily do the ceiling. So that would be — ?" he lifted the paint cans to read the labels "— Biscuit or Dewkist." He burst into laughter. *"Biscuit or dewkist!* Give me a break!" He eyed the can of paint on the floor at Erin's feet. "And the color of the trim paint would be . . . ?"

Erin laughed. "Butterscotch."

David groaned and shook his head. "I had to ask. At least there's no terra-cotta." He gave her a crooked grin and held the bucket of paint in his left hand out to Ted. "I'm guessing you're *biscuit* — whatever that is." He nudged one of the plastic paint trays on the floor forward with his foot. "Pour and roll, pal. Pour and roll."

"That paint's hard to get off." Ted stepped out of the restroom, scrubbing at the back of his hand with a paper towel.

"You were supposed to put it on the walls, not wear it."

140

"Very funny." Ted wadded the towel and threw it at David. "Where's that pizza you ordered?"

A fist pounded against the front door.

"Ah! Just in time!" David tossed the wadded towel he'd caught into a wastebasket, reached into his back pocket for his wallet and went to answer the knock.

" 'Just in time' is right — I'm starved!" Ted glanced at Erin. "We're eating at one of the tables in that big room on the left, right?"

"Right." Erin pulled the door on the storage room closed and started down the hall, stooping to pick up a piece of paper. "Somebody will want this tomorrow! Students are always dropping notes about assigned homework." She jammed it into her pocket and led the way into the room.

"Gather round, people, gather round!" David entered the room, a large, flat cardboard box balanced on one hand, a container of drinks rested on the other. Erin rushed forward and took the drinks before he dropped them. He plopped the box in the middle of a round table and opened the lid. The delicious odor of hot pizza wafted upward, making her mouth water.

Erin set the drinks on the table and accepted the piece of pizza David placed on a paper napkin and held out to her. She smiled, selected a bottle of water and bowed her head to give thanks.

"Yeow! Burning!"

Erin snapped her eyes open.

Ted dropped his piece of pizza on the table, grabbed a soda, popped the cap and took a big gulp. He blew out a gust of air, took another gulp then grinned around the table. "Hot cheese." He fanned his open mouth, panting like a dog in August.

David chuckled. "That'll teach you to wolf down your food." He blew on his piece of pizza and took a bite.

Ted grinned and picked up the piece of pizza he'd dropped. "Not really — I just have to remember to open my soda first next time."

Erin lifted her hand and waved as Ted drove out of the parking lot. The night silence closed in as the sound of the car's motor faded away, but it did little to ease her taut nerves. She was too aware of David standing beside her.

She almost jumped when he reached out and touched her hair.

"A leaf." He glanced down at it. "This yellow color looks nice against your hair." His gaze lifted to fasten on hers. "Did I ever tell you your hair is the first thing I noticed about you?"

Erin shook her head. She didn't have enough breath to speak.

"Well, it was." David smiled and brushed a wisp of her hair off her cheek. "I remember thinking it was the color of chili powder."

Erin forced her lungs to breathe. "Chili powder?" She tried to laugh, to defuse the tension between them. "I thought colors were only red, blue, yellow —"

David laughed, and lowered his hand. "There's that sassy side of you again." He gave her the leaf and opened her car door for her.

Erin slipped behind it, close to the seat, then turned and placed her hands on top of the door. It felt hard, solid, *safe.* Yes, she was beginning to trust David, but she still felt safer with the car door between them. She looked up and gave him a polite smile. "Thanks for helping me tonight, David. Your friends are really nice. My sides are sore from laughing at you and Ted exchanging quips all night. Are you always like that with each other?"

"Pretty much. Ted's a great guy. We've been best friends since grade school. Of course, we do have our serious moments." He grinned. "Just not often. We save that for our work."

His grin was infectious. She returned it. "Well, I haven't seen Ted's work, but yours is certainly wonderful. I can't wait to start scheduling interviews for you with our students. I'll begin talking to them about it tomorrow." She held out her hand. "Thank you for seeing me to my car, David. Good night."

"Good night, Erin. I'll come by tomorrow night to help you paint the second coat." He took her hand in his, then leaned down to lightly press his lips to her temple. "It's late. I'll wait for you to leave before I go. I don't want you here alone."

It happened so quickly she wasn't even sure the kiss was real. Except her heart was pounding so hard she could hear her pulse beating. She nodded.

He squeezed her hand, walked to his car, then turned and lifted his hand in farewell.

Erin climbed into her car, laid the leaf on the seat beside her and reached for the ignition. *David was concerned for her safety.* She glanced out the window as she drove away. He was still standing beside his car, watching her. A wonderful feeling of well-being washed over her. She reached down for the leaf, tucked it into her hair and smiled.

■ ■ ■ ■

Erin eyed her work folder on the bed, sighed and walked to the window. She just couldn't make herself settle down to work. What did that kiss from David mean? A simple thank-you? It was innocent enough — but coupled with the look in his eyes — No! She was being foolish! No matter how nice he seemed, David Carlson was a ladies' man, practiced in flirtation and seduction — just like Alayne's Jerry. He was probably only flirting with her to ensure her cooperation for his big story. She'd do well to keep her mind on business and ignore the way he made her feel.

Erin stood a moment longer, looking out into the night, trying to convince herself she didn't care that David was only using her. Trying to figure out how he had become so important to her. At last she sighed and headed for the closet to get her pajamas. She'd have to be more careful around David.

Erin washed and put cold cream on her face, then pulled off her T-shirt and slipped out of her jeans. Something crackled. She shoved her hand into the right pocket and pulled out the bits of trash she'd picked up to throw away. Among bent paper clips, broken rubber bands and a torn label off a file folder was the slip of paper she'd picked up off the floor. It looked like a memo of some sort.

Erin laid it on the sink, threw the rest of the stuff in the basket, shoved her dirty clothes in the hamper and pulled on her pajamas. The bed was going to feel good tonight! She carried the piece of paper over to the light on the chest by her bed and smoothed the wrinkles from it as best she could. There was a handwritten title at the top of the paper. *Cat and Mouse.* Hmm, that sounded like an interesting assignment. She relaxed back against the headboard and read the memo, seeking the identity of the student or tutor.

September 8 — 4:48 p.m.

Gallo called. There's increased street talk. Wants me to come in for protection till grand jury convenes on Friday. No way!

Gallo chasing V — V chasing me. Who is the cat and who is the mouse?

Cat and Mouse — good title for article when this is over.

David! It was David! He must have dropped the memo when he pulled out his wallet. Erin stared down at the boldly slanted writing. *Gallo chasing V — V chasing me.* A shiver slipped down her spine and spread to her arms and legs. Her hands trembled. She tucked the memo into her work folder, put it on the night table and buried her face in her hands. "Father God, please don't let this evil man, this *V,* hurt David. Keep him safe in Your care, dear God. Please keep David safe in Your care!"

The ring of the phone jolted her upright. She grabbed the handset. "Hello?"

"Hello. I just called to say good night again."

"David!" Erin clutched the receiver close. "Are you all right?"

"Am I — ? Of course, I'm all right. Why? What's wrong, Erin? You sound frightened."

"I *am* frightened!" Erin leaned back against the headboard, pulled her knees up close to her chest and wrapped her free arm around them to stop her shivering. "David, I picked up a piece of paper off the floor at the center and stuck it in my pocket. There was writing on it, and I thought it might be one of the student's notes about an assignment. I just read it." She made an effort to control the trembling in her voice. "It's titled Cat and Mouse."

Silence.

"David, I'm sorry. I didn't mean to read something that wasn't meant for me to see, but —" she closed her eyes and took a breath "— David, are you in danger? Is this . . . this *V* . . . the murderer? Is he after you to — to — ?"

"Hey, hold up, Erin — I'm the writer. I'm the one that's supposed to have the imagination. You're supposed to be a steady, prosaic teacher." David's teasing voice overrode her nervous words. "Listen, Erin, there's nothing to be concerned about. I'm fine. That is except for the lights of the black-and-whites flashing into my bedroom window when they drive by every fifteen minutes."

"Black-and-whites?" Erin relaxed her death grip on the phone and opened her eyes. "There are police cars there?"

"Yes. They've been patrolling around the building as a precaution. I'm perfectly safe. As a matter of fact, I have a cop sleeping on my couch."

"A policeman on your couch! Oh, David —"

"It's nothing, Erin. The D.A. had Detective Gallo assign me a personal bodyguard until after I testify at the grand jury hearing on Friday. He was waiting for me when I got home. That's the other reason I called." There was an indrawn breath. "I'm going to have to break my word about helping you finish up the room tomorrow night, Erin. If there should be a problem, I don't want to endanger you. I'll be staying away until after the hearing. And I want you to forget what you read in that note. Don't discuss any of this with anyone. Okay?"

Erin's throat constricted. He *was* in danger! And he was worried about her!

"Erin? Are you there?"

"I'm here." It came out a whisper.

"Okay, I'll be in touch — Saturday. Don't be concerned if you don't hear from me meanwhile, though I admit I like that you care what happens to me." David's voice softened. "It's late, and you have to be tired from all you did tonight. Thank you again for all your hard work to help me with this story. Good night, Erin."

"Good night, David. And — and please be careful." Erin put the handset back in its cradle, wrapped her arms about her drawn up knees and stared into space. David might be making light of the situation, but the police evidently thought it was serious. The D.A. had ordered protection for him and that meant —

Goose bumps prickled the skin all over

149

her body. *The grand jury would hear the case on Friday.* It was going to be a long four days. Erin closed her eyes, tipped her head down and rested her forehead on her knees. "Dear Lord, please protect David. Please keep him safe, Lord, please. . . ."

Chapter Ten

"Thank you, Mr. Carlson, for your testimony." Brian Sturgis shifted his gaze to the grand jury members. "Are there any questions?"

"I have one." Juror number four crossed his beefy arms over his broad chest and looked at David. "If you were so close and saw the shooter so well, he had to be able to see you, too. Why didn't he shoot *you?*"

There was a hum of murmured approval of the question from the rest of the jurors. David looked squarely into the man's eyes. "Because he never saw me. I saw him through the restaurant window — as I said — but he was intent on his victim." David gestured with his hand. "We were positioned almost the same as Mr. Sturgis and I are now. I can see Mr. Sturgis because he is straight ahead of me, whereas, if he wants to see me he has to turn his head to the right."

There was another murmur of approval — this time for the answer. Brian Sturgis waited a moment, then swept his gaze over the jurors. "Any more questions?"

There were no takers.

"Thank you, Mr. Carlson. And thank you, ladies and gentlemen. . . ."

Thank You, Lord! Thank You, Lord! Thank You, Lord! Erin was almost giddy with relief. David was all right. He had given his testimony before the grand jury yesterday, and Benny Vida had been indicted for murder. It was over. She decided not to think about why that made her so happy, and made a concerted effort to concentrate on her way down the store aisle. "This is fun, Mom. We should go shopping together more often." She held up a turtleneck sweater in a beautiful moss-green color. "What do you think?"

"I think it looks lovely with your hair. Hold it against you." Her mother tilted her head to one side and smiled as Erin complied. "It emphasizes your green eyes. You'll look beautiful in it."

"You wouldn't happen to be prejudiced, would you?"

Her mother laughed. "Perhaps a smidgen."

"Right. A *smidgen.*" Erin grinned and peeked at the price tag, put the sweater back on the shelf and walked to the sales rack, honing in on a wool crepe pantsuit. *David liked blue.* She looked at the label proclaiming the suit machine washable, then slid her hand down and turned over the price tag.

"Yikes! That's a sale price!" Erin snatched her hand back, laughing and shaking it as if she'd been burned. "I think I need emergency care — or rather my purse does. I'm in the wrong store."

"Erin Kelly, behave yourself!" The grin on her mother's face put the lie to her effort to sound stern. She lifted the pantsuit off the rack, draped it over top of the moss-green sweater already on her arm and reached for the inside tag. "Is this the right size?"

"What are you doing, Mom? You said we'd just look. Put those back." Erin reached for the clothes.

"Stop!" Her mother twisted away. "These are for your birthday."

"Oh, really." Erin fought to keep a smile off her face. "My birthday is in April, and this is September, so you're either awfully late or extremely early. Which is it?"

Her mother wrinkled her nose at her — a mannerism Erin recognized only too well as she'd inherited it. "It's a little of both,

153

honey. I find it hard to make up my mind at my age."

So much for outmaneuvering her mom. "Mother —"

"Stop being so prickly and independent, Erin, and let me have my fun. Dad and I know you can take care of yourself." Her mother turned in a slow circle, searching the shop with her gaze. "Where did they move the sports clothes? You need a jacket and pants to go with this sweater." She started off down the aisle.

"Mom!" Erin hurried to catch up. "At least let me carry those."

Her mother gave her a look. "All right. But if you put them back, I'll only get them again and have them delivered." She lowered her head and narrowed her eyes. "I *know* where you live."

Erin laughed at her mom's supposedly threatening tone and took the clothes. "You win."

Her mother grinned. "That's one of the perks of being the mother — I get to win." She stepped over to a rack of pants and started sliding hangers across it, checking for the correct size among the different styles. "I've been meaning to ask you, Erin, are you still seeing Mr. Carlson?"

Erin's lighthearted mood disappeared like

smoke before a strong wind. Her mother's voice was carefully offhand, but she was aware of the concern behind the question. Her parents worried because she'd never come close to having a serious relationship with a man. They understood why — but they worried nonetheless. She tried for a noncommittal answer that would still satisfy them. "Off and on." Her mother pinned her with a look. She gave a little laugh. "All right, it's still business only. We aren't dating, Mom."

Her mother studied her for a moment, then turned her attention back to the clothes rack. "Is it the trust problem? You seem to like him, Erin. There's always a *note* in your voice when you speak of him."

"A *note?*" Erin shook her head. "There's no *note,* Mom. I admire David's work tremendously, and I'm happy to be helping him on an important story, but that's all."

Her mother looked at her — just looked at her.

Erin fought back a sudden urge to duck her head and slink away like a guilty teenager. Did her mother see the attraction to David she couldn't shake off? She sighed. "I do like him, Mom. And I'm beginning to feel comfortable with him. He's very respectful of me. But it is only business."

Tears welled into her mother's eyes. "At least you've found a man you can trust. Even if it is only business, Erin." She gave her a quick hug. "I can't wait to tell your father the Lord has answered our prayers." She turned back to the pants rack. "Speaking of the Lord, is David a Christian, Erin?"

The quiet question hung in the air. She stared at her mother for a long moment, then slowly shook her head. "I don't know, Mom. I've never asked. I told you, our relationship is professional not personal."

Erin looked down and fingered the green sweater draped over her arm. Shopping had lost its appeal. "You know, Mom, I have brown wool pants that will look great with this sweater, let's pay for these clothes and go get something to eat. I'm hungry."

Erin took care of the new clothes, changed into an old comfortable pair of jeans and a loose-fitting cable-knit sweater, shoved up the sleeves and went into the bathroom to brush her mussed-up hair. Troubled, dark green eyes looked back at her from the mirror. A frown knit her brows together. Is this what her mother had seen when she looked at her?

Erin shook her head in disgust at her inability to hide her feelings. She tugged her hair up to the top of her head, secured it with a fabric-covered elastic band then braced her hands on the sink and leaned forward to stare into her own eyes. "So what is the problem, Erin? Why are you troubled about that question your mom asked? What are you afraid of?"

The answer to that question.

Erin shoved away from the sink, hurried through her bedroom into the hall and trotted down the stairs. She grabbed her Bible and notebook off the coffee table and strode straight across the kitchen and out onto the back porch. The screen door slammed shut behind her, the sound shattering the peaceful early evening. A woodchuck that was happily nibbling on fallen fruit from her apple tree jerked his head into the air at the loud bang, then waddled toward the safety of her small garden shed.

Erin watched the small animal disappear in the shed's dark shadow, sucked in a deep breath of crisp autumn-scented air and crossed to the cushioned wicker couch. She'd do what she needed to do, then she'd go pick up those apples before they turned to mush. She folded her body into a pillowed corner, tucked her long jeans-clad legs under her, situated her notebook in her lap and clicked the point down on her pen.

Time to get to work. She lifted her Bible.

You can't avoid the truth.

Erin's face tightened. She wasn't *avoiding* anything, she just had work to do, starting with finding appropriate scriptures for tomorrow's Sunday school lesson.

Yeah! And maybe pigs can fly!

"Stop it!" The words burst out of her mouth, but she might as well have saved her breath; the voice in her head didn't even pause.

Why doesn't David ever mention the Lord? Why doesn't he talk about church or Sunday school? What are you going to do if you ask him if he's a Christian and he says no?

Erin scowled and flipped open her Bible, determined to stop the questions that were swirling through her mind. David's relationship with the Lord was none of her business. He was a business acquaintance, that's all. Now, where was she? She glanced at the header on the page. Amos. She reached out to turn the pages to the book of Acts in the New Testament and her hand paused in midair, her gaze fixed on the verse beside her thumb. "Can two walk together, except they be agreed?"

The words seared into her brain, pierced like a dagger into her heart. Erin snapped her Bible shut, tossed it and the notebook onto the cushion then rose and walked down the back steps, too agitated to sit still. She'd do the Bible work later.

The soles of her sneakers slapped against the brick path as she headed for the garden shed. The bail of the old metal bucket hanging on a nail under the overhang creaked when she took it down.

Erin moved to the apple tree, waved off one of the bees buzzing around and picked up a piece of the rotting fruit. She was getting worked up over nothing. She tossed an apple in the pail then reached for another. Just because David didn't talk about the Lord or anything to do with church didn't mean he wasn't a Christian. He was so wonderful he had to be. He had to be!

If it's only a professional relationship, why is it so important to you? Because if he's not a Christian, that's all it can ever be?

The words rang through her mind, and the truth became clear. For the first time in her life she wanted more than a platonic relationship. For the first time she trusted a man. And if he wasn't a Christian —

Erin bit down on her lip, fighting the desire to burst into tears. She had to face the facts. David was becoming more important to her than she wanted him to be. She didn't want to end up like Alayne. She didn't want to hurt her parents. And she didn't want to disobey the Lord. She dropped the apple and sank to her knees on the lawn, heedless of the rotting fruit and buzzing bees.

"Lord, I don't know how it happened. I didn't want or expect it to happen, but David is the first man I've ever truly trusted or cared about. He's the first man I've felt drawn to. Please make everything all right, Lord. Please make everything all right."

CHAPTER ELEVEN

Erin opened the door and stepped into the back storage room. The faint odor of paint, lingering in the closed-up room, teased her nose. Creamy walls and buttery trim pleased her decorating senses. *Biscuit and butterscotch.*

Erin smiled, thinking of David's reaction to the names of the colors, then wheeled around, picked up the stack of books resting on the low square coffee table outside the door and carried them to the shelves along the side wall. She had to hurry — David would be here for his first interview with a student at four o'clock and she wanted everything to be perfect. She set the books on the shelf, opened the window and went back for more books. When she reached up to place the less popular books on the top shelf, her gaze lifted to the ceiling.

Dewkist — give me a break!

Erin grinned at the memory and ran to

get the small framed pictures she'd bought to put here and there on the shelves to break up the steady line of books. That finished, she went to get the furniture.

She went back to the hall, tipped the coffee table onto its side on the area rug and dragged it into the room. She centered the table on the rug and placed a lamp and an old painted wood carving of a ship's captain she'd picked up at a garage sale on top. She put two chairs from Professor Stiles's office on either side of the table, and moved a third chair to the far wall and set a small wooden TV table beside it. A vase of silk flowers and a couple more books on the tables finished the job. And with a half hour to spare.

Erin gave herself a mental pat on the back and stepped to the doorway to survey her handiwork. *The window!* She hurried out the back door to her car, grabbed the brown, gold and rust plaid curtains off the backseat and ran back inside to hang them with the pressure rod she'd bought on her way home last night. There! The room looked comfortable and welcoming — not at all sterile or businesslike. Drawing a deep breath of relief, she turned and hurried down the hall to her office.

"There's no reason to be nervous, Susan." Erin smiled at the teenager, who stood by the bookshelves gnawing on her lower lip. "Mr. Carlson is a very nice man, and an excellent reporter. Just relax and tell him your story as you've told it to me." Listen to *her* giving advice about relaxing! She was all but hyperventilating at the prospect of seeing David again.

"Yeah, I know." Susan turned her head and looked at her. "It's just — I could get in big trouble with some of my teachers if they ever find out I —" She stopped, her eyes widening, her mouth gaping a bit as her gaze lifted to a point above Erin's head.

Erin fought back a grin. David had that effect on women when they first saw him — she'd witnessed it often. She smiled and turned around. "Come in, Mr. Carlson. You're right on time." She indicated the gaping teenager. "This is Susan Jansen."

"Hello, Ms. Kelly, nice to see you again." David stepped into the room. "Hi, Susan. How are things going at school?"

"Okay, I guess."

"Well, maybe we can make them better than okay."

163

David's smile flashed. Erin caught her breath and closed the door. "That's what we're all hoping." She turned to the bemused teenager. "Susan, you sit at the table with Mr. Carlson. I have some work to do, but I'll be right here if you want me." She crossed to the chair along the wall, sat down and lifted the notebook she'd placed on the TV table into her lap.

She felt David's gaze on her and glanced up. Her pulse quickened as their gazes met. She smiled, then looked down and stared doggedly at the papers she had brought in to correct to keep herself busy during the interview. It was never going to work. She couldn't concentrate. Not with David so near. She kept wanting to look at him.

Erin sighed, reached in the back of the notebook and took out the fashion magazine someone had left on a chair in the tutoring room. It was one of those "what's the latest, hottest style" types of magazines she never bothered with, but at least it would give her something to do. She opened the cover and began flipping through the pages.

Hmm, those pants were nice. A little snug for her taste, but nice. She turned the page. *Wow!* Erin stared at the skimpy sheer top that generously exposed the model's voluptuous breasts and shook her head. How did anyone dare to wear such a thing in public? She glanced at the model's face. She was beautiful. Not that anyone would notice with that outfit she had on.

Erin frowned and turned another page. How could anyone expect teenagers to act in a responsible way regarding physical intimacy before marriage when they encouraged them to dress like —

She stopped, staring at the small picture on the top right corner of the new page. It was the skimpy sheer top model, in an equally skimpy dress, smiling and clinging to a man's arm. The man was David. Erin closed her eyes, took a breath and opened them again to read the caption accompanying the photo.

Brandee Rogers, one of the hottest models in the fashion world today, attended the annual Trends for Those in the Know bash with her hot man-about-town date, David Carlson. Mr. Carlson is a newspaper reporter, so watch what you say around him, ladies.

Man-about-town. Erin closed the magazine, then closed her notebook over the top of it. She couldn't bear to look at it. She felt sick . . . betrayed. She had no right to, but she did. Her estimation of David had been correct all along, though to be fair, he'd never promised her anything. He'd never even asked her out on a date. They only had a professional relationship, just as she'd been telling her mom and Alayne.

Erin took a deep breath to calm the trembling inside her. At least she'd found out she was right about him in time. Before — No. There was no "might have been." There was only her own heedless yielding to David's practiced, seductive charms. *Thank You, Lord. Thank You that I found out the truth about David before I made a complete idiot of myself by falling in love with him.*

Tears that welled into Erin's eyes slipped from under her lashes and slid down her face. She leaned forward to hide her actions and wiped them away. *Help me, Lord. Please help me to get through this interview without betraying my feelings. Please. I don't want David to know how silly I've been.*

"I think that's all I need." David turned off his recorder and smiled at the teenager sitting across from him. "Thank you for sharing your story with me, Susan. I really appreciate it."

There wasn't a trace of nervousness left in the smile Susan gave him. "That's okay, Mr.

Carlson, somebody has to tell it like it really is. I just hope it helps to change things."

"It will help tremendously." David rose as Susan Jansen stood and headed for the door. Erin set aside her notebook and hurried to the teenager's side to usher her out of the room. He gazed after them for a moment, then turned to gather up his things. *One down and —*

"Mr. Carlson?"

David looked over his shoulder, Susan Jansen was peeking around the door frame at him. She looked worried.

"Don't forget —" she gave him a weak smile "— I don't want anyone to know I talked to you."

David grinned. "I won't forget . . . er . . . what's your name again?"

Susan giggled. "Thanks!" The twinkle faded from her eyes. "I wouldn't care, but — I have to graduate, you know. I don't want to get any teachers mad at me." Tears welled into her eyes. She jerked back around the door frame.

Anger spurted through David. Susan was a slow learner, and from his research he'd learned the school she attended "had no funds" for special-needs programs because they chose not to. Under the present administration, children with needs like Susan's were being ignored in favor of extracurricular sports programs that brought in high-achieving students from outlying districts with parents who willingly paid the extra tuition. The slower kids were simply pushed through the system and graduated. It was all about prestige.

"David."

He turned and his heart started thudding at the sight of Erin standing in the doorway.

"Do you think it went well?" She stepped into the room. "Did you get what you needed for your big story?"

David frowned.

"Did I say something wrong?"

He shook his head. "No. It's only that after talking with Susan this isn't about me having a big story anymore." He jammed his tape recorder into his case, snapped it shut and looked at her. "Superintendent Trent and the department of education have a lot to answer for, Erin. I hope that by writing your students' stories I can give them a voice that will be heard, and hopefully — if I do them justice — it will bring about needed change."

Erin stared at him for a long moment, then nodded and turned away. "I'm sure it will."

Her voice sounded different — polite and

distant, without its usual warmth. David frowned and picked up his briefcase as she walked over to the table and retrieved the notebook she'd left there.

"I've another student — the same age as Susan, but from a different school — for you to interview next. Her name is Terri Cooper." Erin brushed her hair back and glanced his way. "She's free every day at this same time, so name your pleasure."

Her eyes looked dull and without their usual sparkle. What was wrong? David studied her face. "I'm busy tomorrow. How about Friday?"

Erin nodded. "I'll call and tell her." She started for the door.

David stepped forward. "Erin."

"Yes?"

Her arm trembled beneath his hand. Concern for her tightened his chest. "You're not coming down with something are you? Because, if so, we can delay —"

"No, I'm not sick, David. I'll schedule the interview for Friday. Good night." She stepped around him and hurried to the back door.

He caught up to her as she shoved it open and stepped out into the dusky night. He fell into step beside her. "What's wrong, Erin?"

"Nothing. I'm just in a hurry to get home." *And throw myself on my bed and cry away this horrible sick feeling.* She quickened her steps and kept walking toward her car.

David lengthened his stride and stepped in front of her, blocking her way. "Erin —"

"Let me pass, David."

Her voice quivered, but was resolute. He shook his head. "Not until you tell me what's wrong. Is it about the interview. Did I — ?"

"The interview was fine. Susan is your newest fan. Now, please, let me by."

The quiver in her voice and the film of tears in her eyes as she looked up at him ripped at David's heart. He reached out and brushed her cheek with his finger. "I'm sorry, but I can't do that. You're upset with me, Erin, at least tell me why. What's the problem? You have to help me here, because I'm at sea as to what is wrong. Have I said or done something — ?"

"Are you a Christian, David?"

Shock spread across his face. Erin looked away. She'd stunned him. She'd stunned *herself,* blurting out a question about his faith like that. But she couldn't very well tell him she felt betrayed by his dating another woman when he hadn't even asked her out on a date! It wasn't his fault she was so pathetic she wanted what he'd never even offered.

Tears threatened. Erin stepped around David and rushed to her car. She wasn't fast enough. He caught her with her hand on the door latch.

"Don't go, Erin. Please." David grasped her upper arms and turned her around to face him. "We have to talk about this."

He took her notebook, laid it on the hood of the car beside his briefcase and grasped her hands. "Look, Erin, I've known all along that you're a Christian and that you hold certain beliefs because of it. And I respect that. I'd never ask you to compromise your beliefs. But the truth is, I don't share them. Nor do I want to. I don't want any part of religion. But I do want the relationship developing between us to grow." His hands tightened on hers. "Is that possible, Erin? Can we get beyond this religion issue?"

Erin felt his words like knives stabbing into her heart. *How had she come so far from the work relationship he was talking about?* She cleared the lump from her throat and nodded. "My faith is an integral part of all that I do, David. You see, being a Christian isn't simply about what I believe, it's who I am. However, this difference in our beliefs will not affect our working together on your story." She withdrew her hands from his, forced her legs to move — to push her back. "I'll call you when I have more appointments sched—"

David's kiss cut off her words. His lips covered hers, the feel of them searing itself into her heart and mind. His arms crushed her against him and the world whirled and dipped until she lost all sense of space and time. And then, he stepped back.

Cold, empty air replaced the warmth and strength of David's body. Erin grabbed for the car to steady herself, lest she collapse in a heap on the ground. The sound of David's footsteps echoed across the concrete, the slam of his car door crashed against her ears. She balled her hands into fists and opened her eyes as his car motor roared to life and his vehicle leaped forward, shot across the empty parking lot and entered the road. She watched until the blurry red dots that were his taillights disappeared, then blinked the tears from her eyes, grabbed her notebook and climbed into her car.

Why did he do that? Why did he have to do that! There was no *reason.* She'd told him she would still help him with his story! Erin snatched her keys from her pocket, snapped on her seat belt and reached for the ignition. Her hand was shaking too hard to fit the key in the slot. Her whole *body* was trembling. She leaned back and closed her eyes, forcing herself to relax.

Why *did* David kiss her? And why was she crying about it? Erin jerked forward and swiped at her tearing eyes. The kiss hadn't even been sweet and gentle. It had been fierce. *Angry* even. As if he truly cared about *her* — not the help she was giving him.

The relationship developing between us.

David's words brought tears flooding back into Erin's eyes. What if he *did* care about her? What if the attraction was mutual? No, that couldn't be. What about his dating the model? It was just his way of enticing her to help him.

Erin snatched the magazine from her notebook. She wasn't going to drive home with that thing in her car! It belonged in the trash! She glared at the magazine and reached for the door handle.

April?

Erin grabbed the magazine with both hands and drew it closer, staring at the date. It was a back issue from April. She hadn't even *met* David in April. She sucked in a breath of air. Why hadn't she thought to check the date before? Why was she so quick to believe the worst about David? She had let her lack of trust in men destroy what might have been. A frisson of hope flickered through her. Unless she explained and asked his forgiveness.

Can two walk together, except they be agreed?

The scripture verse slipped into her mind. The hope died. Fresh pain slammed into Erin. David wasn't a Christian — and he didn't want any part of religion. Even if there was a chance that he was truly attracted to her, there could be nothing between them.

Not now.

Not ever.

He couldn't sleep. David climbed from bed, picked up his phone and walked to the window. His hand twitched from his desire to punch in Erin's number. But he couldn't. There was no way he could overcome a lifetime of resentment against the God who had caused his father to abandon him when he called him to the mission field.

David blew the air from his lungs in a gust of pent up pain. The hurt of his father's rejection had been a part of him for as long as he could remember. The anger had simmered inside him since the day he learned his father had met and married a woman on the mission field, and that neither one of them wanted him because he would get in the way of the *call* God had placed on their lives.

David's chest tightened. Some loving God, who caused a father to turn his back on his own child! He wanted no part of a God who'd do that. He couldn't believe in that sort of God — not even for Erin.

Pain ripped through David's heart, so acute it made him gasp. Anger shook his body. God had taken his mother and grandparents from him through death. He had taken his father from him through the *call* to the mission field. And now God had taken the woman he loved.

CHAPTER TWELVE

"Westwood Literacy Center. Erin Kelly speaking."

"Oh, good, I found you! I took a chance you'd be at the center. Why are you working on this fine October day? I thought you had Saturdays off."

"Hi, Mom!" Erin pushed a bright, happy tone into her voice. "We're really pressed for help so I've been working nights and Saturdays to fill in the gaps." *And to keep from thinking and feeling.*

"So that's why you haven't called this past week — I wondered."

Guilt wormed its insidious way through her. "I'm sorry, Mom. I should have called, but I've been getting home so late . . ." Tears stung Erin's eyes. It was true, but it wasn't the *truth.* She hadn't called because it had been the worst week of her life, and she didn't want her parents to know and suffer with her.

"You sound tired, Erin. Are you getting enough rest? It won't help anyone if you work so hard you become run down and get sick."

Erin's throat tightened at the concern in her mother's voice. She couldn't do this! Just talking to her mom made her want to throw herself in her arms and sob out her misery. "I know, Mom, I'll be careful." She took a breath. "Did you call to chat, or —"

"No. I called to ask you and Mr. Carlson to a casual dinner I'm having tomorrow after church. It's for friends, so he qualifies. I thought two o'clock? Would that be possible? I know it's short notice."

The invitation caught her unprepared. Erin's throat constricted, her chest tightened. She couldn't answer. She sagged back against her chair, closing her eyes. *Help me, Lord. I don't want to cause my mom worry.*

"Erin?"

Lord, help me not to cry! I have to answer her. "No, Mom, it will not be possible. I told you, Mr. Carlson is a only a business acquaintance and —" She took a deep breath. There was one sure way of making sure her mother never did this again. "And David is not a Christian."

"Oh, Erin, I'm so sorry! You must be dreadfully disappointed. Are you all right?"

"Of course, I am." Her voice felt quavery. She had to end this. "I'm really busy, Mom. I have to get back to work. I'll call you tomorrow. I promise."

"No need, Erin. I'll be there in twenty minutes."

"No, Mom, don't —"

Erin looked down at the phone, gently placed it back in the cradle and rose to walk away from her desk. She should have known she couldn't fool her mother. She was making such a *mess* of everything. If only she didn't have to continue to work with David!

Erin hurried out into the empty corridor to go collect the newly updated student address file from Alice's desk, keeping her gaze straight ahead, refusing to look in the direction of the back storage room. She couldn't bear the sight of it. The hardest thing she had ever done was sit through David's interviews. He showed such understanding and sensitivity of the students it was becoming more and more difficult for her to maintain a professional coolness toward him. How was she going to manage the upcoming interviews he would conduct there? Maybe she could double up — schedule two sessions a day and get this torture over with!

David didn't believe in the Lord.

Tears broke through the dam of Erin's willpower. "Lord, please, in Your loving mercy, draw David to You. Don't let him be lost. Draw him. *Draw him* to You, I pray."

He was staring out the window again. David frowned, walked to his desk and closed out the file on his computer. He couldn't concentrate. One minute he'd be working and the next he'd find himself at the window, staring at nothing and thinking about Erin. It had been like that ever since he'd kissed her goodbye and walked away. It had to stop!

"Get out of my head, Erin!" David slammed his fist on the desktop, leaned back in his chair and scrubbed his hands through his hair. How could he get her out of his head when she owned his heart?

When it's right — it's ri—

"Shut up, Ted!" David surged to his feet, stomped out of his study and through the living room then leaped the two steps up into his kitchen. Maybe eating something would distract him. He yanked open the refrigerator door and stared at the empty shelves. No soda. No sandwich fixings. No nothing! He slammed the door shut and searched through the cupboards. Nothing! His normally well-stocked kitchen was bare.

He hadn't felt like grocery shopping lately. Hadn't felt like doing anything. The interviews he'd been conducting had been torture. His life was a mess. Well, that was over right now!

David whirled and grabbed the phone, punched in a number and then hit the disconnect button. He slammed down the phone and walked into the living room.

He was being ridiculous! He scowled, shoved a CD into the stereo and adjusted the sound. Why shouldn't he call Brandee? He didn't owe Erin any allegiance. She wanted no part of him. She made that obvious by the cooly polite way she treated him whenever they were working together.

David's scowl deepened. What was Erin doing right now? Was she at the center working? Or was she out with some of her Christian friends? Did she have someone special in her life? The thought was like a knife to the gut.

David closed his eyes and faced the facts. He didn't belong in Erin's world. He had to get back to making a place for himself in his own. He clenched his hands and stalked back to the phone.

"Hello."

He steeled himself against the ache in his heart. "Hello, yourself."

"David, darling! How wonderful to hear your voice! How have you been?"

"Busy." He blew out a breath. "Look, Brandee, I know this is short notice, but I'm about to go out to dinner and wondered if you'd be free to join me?" He jammed a smile into his voice. "Same deal as before — no strings, just fun and mutual benefit." He drummed his fingers on the counter, waiting while she made up her mind whether to punish him for dropping her or take up where they left off so she could use him for her gain.

"I *do* happen to be free tonight. My date for Carol and Ed's party had to cancel. He's an obstetrician, and he had an emergency." There was a throaty laugh. "I thought dating an OB would sound romantic and heartwarming in the magazines, but it's *so* inconvenient. And he's not half as handsome as you, darling." Brandee's voice purred into his ear. "Let's work a deal. I'll go to dinner with you — you escort me to the party after. Agreed?"

David closed his mind to the calculating shallowness of her words. Who was he to point a finger? He was using her, too. "Absolutely. I'll pick you up at seven?"

"Make it eight. I have to get ready."

Right. He'd forgotten how long Brandee

spent on her appearance. "I'll see you at eight, then. Bye." He hung up on her answering "Byeeeeeee" and walked down the steps to the living room.

He could do this. He could. Brandee might irritate him, but it would be fine as soon as they got to the party and he started visiting with his old crowd. It would be good to get back in the swim of society again.

David rubbed his hand over the back of his neck and rotated his shoulders to loosen his taut muscles. He was getting another headache; he'd had several this past week. That had to stop, too. He frowned and massaged his temples and the tense muscles along his jaw as he headed for the shower.

"It's my own fault, Mom. Alayne warned me that David was a ladies' man, but I had to see him because of the article about the grant for the center and the interviews with the students and other work-related reasons. And he's so wonderful I began to trust him, and then . . . well . . . I just let myself like him too much."

Erin's voice broke. She took a deep breath and looked over at her mother with a silent plea for understanding. "David is everything I want the man I love and marry to be, Mom. He's kind and gentle, intelligent and funny. He's warm and compassionate. He doesn't use coarse language, or indulge in dirty jokes or vulgar conversation — and he likes to play games. He's — he's almost perfect." She took a deep breath and forced out the words. "Except he's not a Christian — and he doesn't want to be one." Her throat squeezed painfully. She blinked moisture from her eyes and rose from her chair.

"Oh, Erin." Her mom reached across the table and gripped her hand. "I'm so sorry for your disappointment and hurt, honey. I wish I could take it away." Her mom squeezed her hand tightly, then leaned back and looked into her eyes. "But I'm afraid this goes beyond a hug and a kiss."

"I know, Mom." It pained her to see the worry and sadness in her mother's eyes and know she'd put it there. Erin stepped back and threw her damp, wadded-up tissue in the wastebasket, determined not to cause her mother any further distress. "Like I said, it's my own fault. I know God's Word warns us not to become involved with unbelievers, and now I know why. No matter how it looks on the surface, at the very core of our being, we're different. And I realize, now, that God's laws aren't for our restriction, they're for our protection." She pasted a smile on her face and walked back to her chair. "I'm sorry, Mom. You and Dad told me that a long time ago, I guess I just had to learn it the hard way."

"Well, it may not be much comfort at the moment, Erin, but believe me, you're not alone. None of us are perfect. The Lord is still working on us all." Her mother reached over and took hold of both her hands. "Let's pray for David."

"I'll tell you how she got her face on the cover! She spent a few nights at the cabin with the director of the agency, that's how!"

"Really! That *conniving* —"

David pivoted on his heel and walked away from Brandee's side. Dinner had been a disaster, and the party was turning out to be the same. All Brandee talked about was how much prettier and sexier she was than the other models. And her claws *really* came out when she learned one of them had gotten a cover or shoot she coveted. Erin never tore down other —

Stop it! Stop thinking of Erin! David frowned and turned his attention to a small cluster of people listening intently to the man they surrounded. Maybe their conversation would interest him. He walked over to join them, arriving midway through some amusing story.

The small crowd of people suddenly roared with laughter. An off-color joke — he should have known. David backed away.

"Why the scowl, handsome? Did your date leave you high and dry . . . I hope." David looked down and met a blatant invitation in a pair of hazel-colored eyes. A pouty, lipstick-coated mouth curved into a "hello there" smile as the woman placed her carefully manicured hand against his chest. "Hmm, nice." The smile warmed, but there was a glimmer of shrewd alertness in the eyes. "You're David Carlson, the reporter who does feature articles for *The Herald,* aren't you?" Long, tapered fingers trailed down his shirtfront. "I could give you a story."

David jerked back, repulsed by the woman's suggestive tone. "Excuse me. I have an appointment elsewhere." He could feel the woman staring after him as he wound his way through the milling crowd toward Brandee.

"Champagne, sir?"

David stopped and glanced at the fancy half-full flutes on the silver tray being held by a hired waiter. He hadn't had a drink since he met Erin. His face muscles went taut. That was over, and he needed *some-*

thing to help him get through this party. He lifted a drink from the tray and went to stand against the wall, surveying the room. Every woman at the party had a bare minimum of cloth covering her, and every famous, wealthy, powerful or influential man there was ogling, leering and touching with abandon.

David's stomach curled in on itself. He couldn't hear their conversations but he didn't have to. He knew from his own experiences at gatherings like these what was taking place — false flattery and outright lies leading to assignations and deals that would advance careers and generate wealth. He'd done it himself often enough, but it thoroughly disgusted him tonight. Why?

I don't lie. If I'd only wanted to say something complimentary to "stroke your ego," I'd have told you I like your tie —

The revulsion David was feeling spiked at the memory of Erin's words. Erin. The mere thought of her was like a breath of fresh air in this polluted atmosphere. It would take more than a drink to make the scene palatable.

David swept his gaze to Brandee, and his stomach clenched so hard that he almost lost the little dinner he'd been able to force down. Ronald Deerling, owner of Models Inc., stood close beside her, staring down at her décolletage while his hand caressed the flesh bared by the low-cut vee in the back of her dress. She was smiling up at him.

That did it! David lurched away from the wall, slammed his untouched drink down on a table and stalked to Brandee's side. "Something's come up. I'm leaving. Do you want to come along? Or —"

"Why don't you stay with me, babe?" Ronald Deerling glanced at him. "I'll take care of Brandee."

David almost gagged. He shifted his gaze to her face. "Brandee?"

She smiled and slipped her arm around the paunchy waist of the elderly, balding Ronald. "I'll stay."

Relief surged through David. He'd had all he could take of her tonight. "Suit yourself. *Goodbye,* Brandee."

Her eyes sparked with anger. She'd understood his message — *goodbye* instead of good night. If she hadn't been holding a drink in one hand and the pudgy Ronald with the other, she'd probably have slapped him. It would have been worth it to be free of her again. He'd been out of his mind to call her — to come here with her.

David turned and walked out of the

house, taking a long deep breath of the clean night air. *What now?* He scowled and climbed into his car. He didn't want to face another long, lonely night — especially Saturday night. But he'd had his fill of his old crowd. He couldn't stomach seeing them again — *literally.* Maybe Ted and Darlene . . .

David grabbed his cell phone, stared at it. He didn't really want to see Ted and Darlene, either. He didn't relish the idea of being around a lovey-dovey engaged couple. Erin had spoiled that for him, too.

He threw his cell phone onto the passenger seat, jammed the car into gear and drove out of the parking lot. He'd find *something* to do that — a movie! Yeah, that was it; he'd go to a movie. He glanced at the clock on the dash and nodded with satisfaction. He could catch the late show. He flipped on his signal, turned onto Truman Boulevard and headed for the theater.

CHAPTER THIRTEEN

Erin took one last swipe at her eyes with the tissue and pushed the swinging door open far enough to slip through into the sanctuary. She was tired of crying, but her emotions were raw and thinking of David had brought on another spate of tears.

Erin tiptoed to the empty back pew. She'd been hiding in her classroom until the concern and question provoking flood was over, and now she was late for church. Pastor Ryan was already preaching his sermon. At least she was finally cried out! She sighed, put her notebook down, glanced at the posted Scripture references and opened her Bible.

". . . and my point is — it's not always easy to do the right thing, and sometimes we fall into temptation."

Erin's heart lurched. She jerked her head up and stared at the pastor.

"And I know what I'm talking about. You

may find this hard to believe, but I haven't always been perfect." Laughter swept the congregation. Pastor Ryan grinned, then stepped back behind the podium. "I've struggled with temptations in the past, and I'm sure I'll struggle with more in the future. I'm human. We all are."

The pastor swept his gaze over the congregation and Erin wanted to slink under the pew. It felt as if she had a banner with the word *guilty* in big block letters waving over her head. *Is this how Alayne felt? Was this why she wouldn't come see —*

"The good news is God knows that. He's aware of our human weakness and He gave us the answer for it. That's why Jesus said to Peter, 'Watch and pray, that ye enter not into temptation — the spirit indeed is willing, but the flesh is weak.'"

Conviction burned in Erin's heart. She hadn't watched or prayed as she should have when David came into her life. Quite the opposite. She had ignored the inner warnings she felt. *Lord, forgive me for not watching and praying as I should have — for wanting my will instead of seeking Yours.*

". . . here to tell you, it's *hard* when we go against the spirit and yield to the flesh. Disobedience is sin, and sin has a price. The Bible says, The wages of sin are death." The

190

pastor's gaze swept the congregation again. "That could be a death in the circumstance. For instance, if the sin is a physical one, it can be good health that dies. If it's lying, trust can die. If it's cheating, a relationship may die. But ultimately sin brings *spiritual* death — an eternity spent separate from God. None of us wants that. And being the loving, merciful Father He is, God doesn't want that, either. He *loves* us. And He wants us with Him always."

Erin caught her breath as Pastor Ryan gripped the sides of the podium and leaned forward. "That's why, when we've done something we know is wrong, when we have sinned, the best thing we can do is run to God. Run *to* Him. Not *from* Him. We need to ask His forgiveness, receive it, then 'go and sin no more.' "

The words settled into her heart. Erin bowed her head and closed her eyes. *Father God, I was wrong to ignore Your Word and the warning voice You placed inside me — and I'm sorry. I'm so sorry, Father. Please forgive me for not obeying You.*

". . . and remember, Psalms, chapter thirty, verse five says, 'For his anger endureth but a moment; in his favor is life: weeping may endure for a night, but joy cometh in the morning.' "

Tears stung Erin's eyes. *Thank You, Lord, for Your divine favor. And for the joy that will be mine again someday.*

The pastor straightened and walked to the front of the platform. "God loves us. So when we stray from what we know is right, when we ignore His Word and go our own way, let's run back to His loving arms, confess our sin and let His forgiveness and love wash us clean so that our fellowship with Him will be sweet and eternal. Let us pray."

Erin swallowed back the tears, bowed her head and let God's forgiving, redeeming grace flow through her.

Erin leaned back against the soft pillow on the couch and closed her eyes, thinking about Pastor Ryan's message. *Go and sin no more.* The words were confirmation that she had done the right thing in turning away from David. It didn't take the hurt away, but it brought her a measure of inner peace. Making a clean breast of things with her mom yesterday had helped, also. Her mother's prayers for her healing, and for David's salvation, gave her a good deal of comfort.

Erin smiled and brushed back a stray lock of hair. God was no respecter of persons — His word said so — but just the same, she always felt better when her mother prayed with her for something. It was a holdover from her childhood. As a young girl, she'd been certain God always listened to her mother and did what she asked, and her mom had never disabused her of that notion. Her smile widened. Her mother was a very smart woman.

The ring of the phone interrupted her musings. Erin glanced at her watch and winced at the ache that shot through her. Two o'clock — the time her parents had planned to have the dinner to meet David. It was probably her mom calling to see if she was all right. She sighed and picked up the receiver. "Hello."

"Boots! What are you doing home?" There was a quick breath. "I mean, it's Sunday afternoon. I figured you'd be at Mom and Dad's, or —"

"No, I'm home." Erin jumped in to change the subject — she just couldn't deal with any more negative things at the moment, and she and her sister didn't see eye to eye on the way you should treat your parents. "I'm glad you called, Alayne. I haven't talked with you since you came home from your trip with Jerry. I've only had that one message you left on my machine saying you were back."

"I've been busy."

"Oh?" Erin sat up a little straighter. Alayne sounded odd. And why was she calling when she thought she wouldn't be home? "Lots of bones being broken lately?"

"Not exactly." There was a pause. "I quit my job. I'm not working for Dr. Swan anymore."

"You quit! Why?" *Jerry's affair with Dr. Swan's receptionist.*

"That's what I called to tell you, Boots. I'm moving — leaving town."

Erin jerked forward on the couch. "Leaving town! Why? Did Jerry get a promo—"

"It has nothing to do with Jerry. We're through. He's scum! I caught him cheating on me again."

Again. Erin's hand clenched on the phone. Alayne's voice had sharpened, but she could hear the hurt underneath her sister's anger and it made her blood boil. She'd like five minutes alone with Jerry Burdick! "I'm sorry, Alayne, I . . . Are you all right?"

"No. But I will be. I'm a survivor. You know that, Boots."

"Alayne, don't try to get through this by yourself." Erin's heart contracted with empathy. The pain of giving up hope of a relationship with David was terrible, and she'd only known him a few months. Her

194

sister had been with Jerry for seven years. She gripped the phone tighter. "Alayne, why don't you come over and we can talk about this? I know how you feel and —"

"Don't ask, Boots. I can't do that, especially now. Look —" there was a crackle of static "— I'm getting out of range, I've got to go. I'll call you when I get settled somewhere."

Erin shot to her feet. "*Settled somewhere?* You don't know where you're going?"

"No. I'm just heading west."

"Heading — You mean you're leaving right *now!* Alayne, *wait!*" Erin grabbed her car keys off the coffee table, stuffed her feet into her backless sneakers and ran for the front door. "If you won't come here, I'll meet you somewhere. Anywhere you say! You can't just —"

"Too late. Here's the interstate access ramp. Bye, Boots. I love you."

"*No!* Alayne, I love you, too! Please don't —" Erin winced as the phone went dead "— go."

It was too much. Her fragile peace shattered. Erin threw the phone onto the couch and lifted her face toward the ceiling, the car keys biting into the soft flesh of her right palm as she clenched her hands into fists. "Lord, I've been praying that You would draw Alayne back to You and restore her to our family for seven years. And now look what's happened! She's running away. She's *running away,* Lord! And I don't know if I'll ever see my big sister again!"

Tears streamed down her face. Erin hurled the car keys toward the coffee table. She missed. She stared at the keys gleaming on the carpet, took a deep breath, wiped the tears from her face and walked over to pick them up. Having a tantrum wouldn't help. Nothing would. Alayne would still be gone, and she would still have to go tell their mom and dad.

Tears flowed again. Erin swiped them away and headed for the door, bracing herself for the ordeal ahead.

"You shouldn't talk so much, pal, you wear a guy's ears out."

"Sorry." David glanced over at Ted and forced a grin. "I guess I'm not my usual ebullient self."

"Yeah, I noticed." Ted took a swallow of his water. "As a scintillating dinner conversationalist you leave a lot to be desired." He put down his glass and fixed David with an assessing gaze. "This break with Erin has really hit you hard. You're down for the count, Dave. I've never seen you so low. Are you sure —"

"Don't go there, Ted!" His friend's eyebrows shot up. David took the snap and growl out of his voice. "Sorry. I just don't want to talk about it."

Ted nodded and cut off a bite of steak. "Whatever you say, but it might help to get Erin out of your system."

David shot him a look. "You make her sound like some sort of drug. She's not in my *system* — she's in my heart and mind and I can't get her out!" He threw down his fork and shoved his barely touched meal aside, motioning their server for coffee. "She'd be everything I ever wanted if she wasn't a Christian."

Ted snorted. "It would take me two seconds to tear *that* bit of flawed reasoning to shreds in a courtroom."

David bristled. "Flawed reasoning! How so?"

"It makes no sense." Ted ate his bite of meat while the server filled their cups, then put down his fork and picked up his spoon as she walked away.

David scowled at him. "Well, O *master of deduction,* are you just going to leave me hanging here, twisting in the wind? Or are you going to explain where I erred in my thinking?"

Ted grinned, added a spoonful of sugar to his black coffee and stirred. "It's simple, O *needy one.* Our beliefs and experiences make us who we are. You fell in love with Erin *because* she's a Christian, Dave, not in spite of it."

"That's ridiculous!"

"Is it?" Ted put down his spoon and fastened his gaze on him. "It's why Darlene and I are so fond of her. She's different than all our other friends and we like that difference. In fact, we've decided to do something about it." He picked up his cup.

David straightened in his chair. "And what would that be?"

Ted swallowed a mouthful of coffee and set his cup back on its saucer. "There's something beautiful and *special* deep inside Erin that springs from her being a Christian, Dave. You know it, and I know it. Darlene and I want whatever that is. We decided the best way to get it is to find out what church Erin goes to and start attending."

"*You're* going to *church?*" David flushed as the patrons at the nearby tables glanced their way. He lowered his voice. "I don't believe it. What about your living situation?"

"Darlene and I had a long discussion about that. The upshot was, Darlene moved into her parents' house. She's going to stay there until our wedding next month."

"What?" David gaped at him.

Ted nodded. "I know. Unbelievable, isn't it? But we're dead serious about this. We want to get our lives on track and start our marriage off right." He leaned forward, every trace of amusement gone from his eyes and face. "Why don't you come to church with us, Dave?"

David stiffened. "Not interested."

Ted fixed him with his "lawyer's look." "Are you sure? 'Cause you certainly aren't happy with the way things are."

David could have punched him. It was true. He *wasn't* happy. He wasn't even *content.* His old girlfriend seemed jaded and coarse; he couldn't stomach his old friends' behavior; and his single-minded desire for fame as a top reporter with its accompanying opportunities for wealth had dimmed considerably in the past few weeks. He had to get his life back on track!

"I'm sure, Ted. But thanks for the invite. *And* for helping me figure out what's wrong and how to fix it." He threw his napkin down on the table. "Now, if you'll excuse me, I've work to do. There's a series of stories waiting to be written with my name on them." David shoved back his chair, rose, pulled out his wallet and threw some bills on the table to cover the cost of his meal.

"What? No dessert?" Ted's eyes widened in feigned shock, and he shot a pointed look at David's uneaten food.

David glowered at him. "You're enjoying this way too much, buddy. Have fun in church next Sunday!" He tucked his wallet back in his pocket, shoved his chair under the table and walked away.

David pulled into his allotted parking space, killed the motor and climbed from the car. Ted was going to church. *Ted!* Of all people. He couldn't believe it. He locked the car and started for the door, the keys in his hand jiggling an accompaniment to his swirling thoughts. His whole world had turned upside down since he'd met Erin, but it was going to stop! He was going to start focusing on his career again. If he —

"Don't you ever look around you, Carlson?"

David jerked to a halt, glancing in the direction of the familiar gravely voice. "What are you doing here, Gallo? It's Sunday. Don't they ever give you a day off?"

The detective pushed away from the cement pillar he was leaning against and stepped toward him. "It is my day off. Answer my question."

David frowned. He was in no mood to play games. "You answer mine. What are you doing here?"

"Just looking things over." Don Gallo swept his gaze over the parking garage and a look of disgust spread across his chiseled features. "Every slot labeled with the corresponding apartment number — nothing like making life easy for someone who wants to find you." His gaze traveled back to him. "You always park in the same spot, Dave?"

"That's the general idea. It saves arguments with my neighbors."

"Yeah? Well, it can get you killed, too."

David's frown matured into a scowl. "I thought things had quieted down since the grand jury hearing. Are you picking up new rumblings about me on the streets?"

"No. That's what worries me. Things have gotten too quiet. Information has dried up. It takes power to shut people's mouths like that." Gallo shoved his hands in his coat pockets. "I've had orders to call off the black-and-whites because I've got nothing new — not even a rumor — to justify the time and expense of them patrolling around here any longer. I'll reinstate the patrols two weeks before the trial, but until then you're going to be on your own."

David studied Gallo's impassive face. "All

right. Thanks for the warning." He turned toward the door.

"You need to vary your routine, Carlson. Don't go to the paper at the same time, and don't go there every day. Better yet, work at home the way you did before the grand jury session. Don't park in the same places all the time, there or here. Stay away from the gym." Gallo's face darkened. "I could set my watch by your schedule there. And in the name of all that's holy, look around you once in a while!"

David glowered at him. "Have you been *following* me?" He wasn't happy at the thought, and he didn't bother to hide it.

Gallo shrugged. "Long enough to know you need to make some major changes in the way you do things."

David stared at him. The man wasn't even ruffled by his displeasure. "Look, Gallo. I appreciate the advice, but I have to live my life. And there's nothing I can do about the parking — it's illegal on the street. So unless you want to fix my tickets, this is it."

"Then stay alert. Mark the places someone could hide in here and drive around and check them all before you park and turn off your engine. You climbed from your car without so much as a glance at me."

"I was thinking about something."

"Well, the next time, wait until you get inside to do your thinking!" The detective walked to his car, opened the door then looked at him. "The black-and-whites are gone, Carlson. Nobody's got your back. Be careful. And keep your cell phone in your hand with your thumb on my number when you're walking around. Punch it if you're in trouble, even if you can't talk. I can trace the call and find your location. Now, get inside." Gallo slid in his car and drove away.

David stared after the detective, then shook his head and unlocked the door. What else could go wrong? His life was a mess! A total mess! He jabbed the up button for the elevator, then took a long, careful survey of the entrance hall while he waited for the elevator to arrive.

Chapter Fourteen

David stepped into his small entrance hall, tossed his car keys into the brass bowl on the red-lacquered chest and loosened his tie as he descended the two steps into the living room. The place felt lonely, but there was nowhere else to go at this hour. He wasn't into bars.

He yawned, flipped on the lights then threw his tie over the back of one of the wood chairs surrounding his dining table as he walked by. He'd been working from dawn to midnight or later every day for the past two weeks and he still couldn't sleep. Every time he closed his eyes he saw Erin's face. He woke up to the same image. And the loneliness increased. It was worst here at home.

David scowled, undid the collar button on his dress shirt and stepped up into the kitchen to get a can of tomato juice from the refrigerator. He popped the top and took a swig. Why should that be? Erin had never been here. Of course, she'd never been at his office at *The Herald,* either, and he felt the same emptiness there. He carried it around in his heart. The only time he felt whole was when he was at the center conducting interviews and she was there in the room. But, of course, that was torture! And it was getting worse instead of better. He'd almost lost it today. If Professor Stiles hadn't come in —

David glanced at his reflection in the dark window over his sink and lifted the can in a mock salute. "Here's to your pathetic self, buddy!" He chugged a couple more swallows of the drink, set the can on the counter and went back into the living room to punch the play button on his answering machine. If he was lucky, it would be a spokesperson telling him he'd won a week's cruise aboard a luxury liner. That would take him away from all his —

"Hello, David, it's Erin."

The sound of her voice slammed into him like a sucker punch to his gut. He inhaled a quick breath.

"I'm calling to tell you that Janet Wallace has to cancel her interview with you tomorrow. Her little girl has taken ill. So . . . a moment please."

There was an indrawn breath, then total silence. She'd covered the phone. Had there been a quiver in that breath? Or was he imagin—

"Sorry. As I was saying, her little girl is ill so tomorrow is out and Janet can't come next week. We'll have to reschedule."

She'd made her voice brisk, businesslike. But it stirred his heart just to hear her speak. "Let me know dates and times when you're free and I'll —"

David didn't wait to hear the rest. He spun on his heel, ran to the chest, scooped up his car keys and slammed out the door. *Enough was enough! He'd been a fool to walk away from Erin! There had to be some way to work this out!* He bolted by the slow elevator and dashed down the stairs, shoving his way through the security doors on each floor to reach the parking garage.

David's heart thudded in rhythm with his pounding feet as he raced to his car. His fingers fumbled as he jammed and twisted the key in the ignition. The roar of his car motor shattered the silence, the sound bouncing off the concrete walls as he yanked the gear shift into Reverse. He backed out of his parking slot, then shot up the ramp to exit the garage.

■ ■ ■ ■

He made it in eighteen minutes. David pulled to the curb, his gaze fastened on Erin's house. The lights were on. She was still awake. He killed the motor and jerked from the car. And then he remembered her words.

Being a Christian isn't simply about what I believe, it's who I am.

The truth thrust into his heart like a blade, freezing him in place. There was no way to compromise — to work this out. Erin's faith was who she was. The hope that had driven him to find her died. David tightened his grip on the car door and slid back into his seat. Erin wouldn't see him on a personal basis. She wouldn't let a relationship develop between them. He suddenly knew that more surely than he knew his own name — and the knowledge brought him face-to-face with his own truth.

Pressure built in his chest. David closed the door, gripped the wheel then leaned back and shut his eyes, trying to take a normal breath. Erin was the only woman he'd ever loved — ever wanted to spend his life with — and he couldn't have her. There was no hope for them. She wouldn't compromise her beliefs, and he didn't have any.

The pressure increased. David sucked in air, blew it out and looked across the street. "I love you, Erin. I'll always love you." His whispered words bounced off the window glass and lost themselves in the interior of the car. It didn't matter. The words were useless without Erin to receive them. He braced himself against the agony of hurt inside, started the car and drove away.

Erin lifted her head, listening. For what? The only sound that broke the silence was a car stopping outside. She tensed, waiting for the slamming of a car door then sighed and shook her head. How sad that the only excitement in her life was her neighbor's comings and goings. She glanced down at the book in her hands and laid it aside. Chapter four, and she didn't have a clue as to what the story was about — she was only reading words.

Erin heaved another sigh, rose from the couch and went on tiptoe to stretch the kinks from her body by pushing her arms straight overhead. A car started outside. She walked toward the window, then hung back as a cat, carrying some sort of animal in its mouth, walked into the splotch of gold the streetlight threw onto her front lawn. "Eeeww! Take that home, kitty. Don't leave it in my yard."

Her words sounded stark, *lonely* in the quiet of the living room. Erin frowned, walked to the armoire standing against the far wall and slid a CD into the player. She would be so glad when this hollow ache that had replaced the first raw pain of turning away from David was gone. It was terrible. She felt only half alive, as if her heart was missing. And now there would be another week of interviews to sit through.

"*Stop it!* Stop mooning about feeling sorry for yourself, Erin Kelly. Go do something!" She winced and looked up at the ceiling. "Do you hear that, Lord? I'm reduced to talking to myself."

Light from a moving car poured through the front window, throwing her shadow against the wall. She turned and looked at the front door, then — spurred by an impulse she couldn't explain — ran over to pull the door open and step out on the porch.

Erin scanned the immediate area, then frowned and trotted down the steps to the sidewalk to look up and down the street. The only thing in sight were the tiny red dots of a car's taillights in the distance.

Breathless, agitated, her heart pounding

like a trip hammer, she retraced her steps to the house. What on earth was wrong with her, running outside for no reason? She was losing her mind!

Erin climbed the steps, reached for the door handle then stopped and walked over to plop down on the swing, wrapping her arms around herself to stop the shivers brought on by the cold night air. She didn't want go back in the house yet — though she had no idea why.

She pushed her toes against the porch floor, setting the swing in motion. Where was Alayne? And where was David? At home sleeping, or out tracking down a story?

The hurt in Erin's heart swelled. It always did when she thought of David. She sighed, closed her eyes and began to pray.

The road ended. David jerked out of his ruminations, staring in confusion at the crossroad in front of him. Where was he? He swept his gaze over the unfamiliar rural landscape. No markers. No road signs. He opened the car door, stepped outside and looked back the way he had come. The narrow country road disappeared into darkness.

He frowned and glanced back at the

crossroad. What an idiot to drive around without paying attention to where he was going! Well, he had to make a choice. He got back in the car, grabbed a quarter from the change dispenser in the console and flipped it into the air. "Heads, I go right." He caught the coin and slapped it onto the back of his other hand. *Heads.*

The interior light went off. David put the quarter back in its slot, shifted into gear and turned right. The road had to come out somewhere. Good thing he always kept his gas tank full.

Welcome To Havenbrook.

David stared at the sign lit by his headlights. At last! Someone in this town should be able to put him back on the road to home. He cruised by a stone building sporting a sign that declared it to be Harvey's Repair Shop. Across the street was a gas station. Handy. Harvey was probably their best customer — when the station was open, that is.

David shot a look at his gas gauge — *still half full* — and drove on past several old-style houses. His heart jolted with painful memory as he swept around a curve and spotted a gazebo in the center of a small park that formed the town's circle. An image of Erin shaking raindrops from her hair flowed into his mind. His hands clenched on the wheel.

He drove slowly into the circle, studying the stores around the outer edge. A restaurant that touted Patsy's home cooking came into view on his right. Good thing he wasn't hungry, because there was no sign of Patsy or anyone else. Just as well, his stomach rebelled at the thought of food. Still, he needed directions. Where was everyone?

David glanced down at the dash. One o'clock in the morning. No wonder everything was closed. Now, what should he do? He looked back up and eased the pressure of his foot on the accelerator. On the corner of the road leading out of the circle was a small white clapboard church, its stained-glass windows glowing with soft luminance. A lamppost in the tiny yard threw light into the darkness, highlighting a stone path that led to the front door of an attached ell. He could see a man sitting at a desk inside.

Being a Christian isn't simply about what I believe, it's who I am. Erin's words echoed in his mind. David pulled over to edge of the road and stopped, staring out his windshield at the church. *You fell in love with Erin because she's a Christian, Dave, not in spite of it.*

David lifted his hand and rubbed his forehead. Was Ted right? There was no denying that his outlook on a lot of things had changed to reflect Christian values. Was he only being stubborn in refusing to accept them as his own to get back at his father for rejecting him as a child? Was he missing out on the best thing that could ever happen to a person because of his past?

You'll never know unless you open yourself to the truth. You're a reporter — investigate. Go knock on the door.

David ran his hand over the taut muscles at the back of his neck, then reached down and switched off the ignition. If he changed his mind, he could always tell the pastor — or whoever he was — he was lost and needed directions home. It was the truth. He opened the door and got out of the car. His footsteps were the only sound that broke the night's silence as he walked up the path toward the welcoming light.

Erin dropped the last spoonful of dough on the cookie sheet, slid it in the oven and set the timer. She rinsed the bowls and cooking utensils under hot tap water, loaded them into the dishwasher, wiped up the counter and dried her hands on a paper towel. Four minutes to go on the timer — long enough.

She went into the living room to put a book back on the shelf, fluffed the couch pillows, carried her shoes to the stairs and returned to the kitchen just as the buzzer sounded. The cookies were done. The house was in order. Now what? She was cried out, prayed out, and more physically tired than she had ever been, but she wasn't sleepy.

Erin yawned as she picked up the spatula and slid the cookies off the baking sheet onto the counter to cool. She took care of the dishes and went back to the living room. Her eyes burned. She loaded in three more CDs, picked up her shoes and trudged barefoot up the stairs. The piano stylings of Ferrante and Teicher surrounded her as she changed into her pajamas and flopped down on her bed.

She slanted a look toward her nightstand, reading the digital numbers glowing there in the dark. Three o'clock. Only four more hours to get through before she could get up and get ready for work. She gave a deep sigh, turned onto her side and stared at the darkness outside the window.

CHAPTER FIFTEEN

"David."

He almost dropped his briefcase. He thought she'd gone. He turned and looked at Erin. She was standing in the doorway, as if she didn't trust herself alone in the same room with him. Just as well with the way his heart was hammering against his ribs at the sight of her.

"I just wanted to thank you again for the stories you're writing. Our students are very excited about them." Her eyes glowed with admiration. "You do an amazing job of capturing their frustration and helplessness, yet you always end with a solution that gives hope." She smiled, her lips slightly trembling, and he ached to pull her into his arms and hold her close. "We're all on pins and needles wondering what fruit they'll bear. The young ones say all their parents and teachers are discussing them."

"That's good to hear. And I'm sure you'll

be pleased to know the paper is getting a lot of favorable response." He looked away from the faint purple circles under Erin's eyes that betrayed her sleepless nights and fastened his gaze full on hers. "How are you, Erin?"

She looked away, but not before he saw the unhappiness in her eyes. "I'm . . . improving." She took a deep breath and cleared her throat. "How about you?"

"Well, I could lie and tell you I'm fine —" David cleared his own throat and took a step toward her "— but the truth is —"

Erin raised her hand — palm out — between them, stopping him in his tracks, halting his words. "Please don't come closer, David, and don't say anything more. I only came back to tell you I've scheduled your next interview for six-thirty Friday night."

Before he could say another word, she hurried away.

David charged toward the door, then stopped. He'd already made one mistake — he didn't need to compound it. *Stupid, clumsy oaf!* You certainly bungled that! He scrubbed his hand over the nape of his neck and walked out into the hallway. Erin's office door was shut — closing him out. But not for long. Only until tomorrow night.

Because he knew now that in spite of his idiotic stubbornness about religion she cared about him.

David's lips curved into a smile. He wanted to go break down Erin's door and tell her what had happened to him. How his heart had changed since they'd been apart, but he had the final step to take first. And he was ready — he knew he was. Tonight, when he drove to Havenbrook for his lesson with Pastor Gardner, he was going to give himself, heart and soul, to the Lord.

"Therefore if any man be in Christ, he is a new creature: old things are passed away; behold, all things are become new." David quoted the verse under his breath. When he'd read it this morning he'd known that was what he wanted. He wasn't interested in his old way of life any longer. More than anything he wanted to be born again — to become a new man in Christ.

David glanced at his watch and hurried toward the back door. It was five-thirty. He just had time to drop tomorrow's article off at *The Herald* before driving to Havenbrook. He reached for the doorknob and glanced over his shoulder at Erin's closed door. *I'm coming back a new man in Christ, tomorrow night, Erin. And then I'm going to win your heart and nothing will ever separate us again.*

Erin threw her sandwich in the trash. She couldn't eat. Seeing David almost every day was agony. And it wasn't getting any better. She was going to have to go to Professor Stiles tomorrow and tell him she couldn't sit in on the interviews anymore.

Her stomach churned. Erin leaned against the counter and closed her eyes. She couldn't do that. The professor had made her presence at the interviews a condition of the center's involvement. If she backed out, David would lose the basis for his series, the students would lose their voice and the education department abuses would go on as always.

Tears squeezed from under her eyelids. "Oh, Lord, I know it's my own fault that I've brought this hurt on myself. But please help me be strong for the sake of all the children whose education is being neglected."

The ring of the phone jolted her out of her prayer. Erin wiped away her tears and reached for the handset. "Hello."

"Hi, Boots."

"Alayne!" Erin cradled the phone closer to her ear and headed for the living room. "I'm so glad you called. Are you all right?

218

Where are you now?"

"I'm fine. I'm in Iowa."

"But that's so far!"

"Not far enough. Jerry travels this far west for his company. I want to be someplace he's never been."

Erin's heart squeezed at the bitterness in Alayne's voice. "Where's that?"

"I'm not sure — I'm thinking Colorado."

Erin sank onto the couch a visual map of the United States in her mind. Her throat tightened. *Lord, she's my only sister, and we'll be so far apart.*

"Boots?"

Erin swallowed hard. "I'm here."

"Look, Boots, I've got to get something to eat and make my travel plans for tomorrow. I only wanted to let you know I'm okay. Tell Mom and Dad for me. I'll call again in a couple of days. Bye."

Erin knew arguing or begging Alayne to call their parents herself was fruitless. She let out a tired sigh. "All right. I'll call them. Drive careful, Alayne. I love you."

"I love you, too, Boots."

The phone went dead. Erin stared at it for a long moment, then tossed it onto the cushion beside her, leaned her head back and closed her eyes. She had to break the news of Alayne's continuing to travel to her

219

mother and father, but she wanted to wait until Alayne had settled somewhere. The very thought of telling them she was so far away made her ill. Her own behavior had hurt them enough. But at least she hadn't run away. That didn't solve anything. The hurt just went with you. Better to face your problem, confess your fault and receive forgiveness.

"For his anger endureth but a moment; in his favor is life: weeping may endure for a night, but joy cometh in the morning."

The words brought peace to her aching heart. "Thank You, Lord, for Your word. I believe in Your truth. And though I may cry tonight, I believe that, by Your grace, I will have joy tomorrow."

CHAPTER SIXTEEN

David lifted his gaze to the dark night outside his bedroom window and smiled. Two weeks ago he'd have been complaining about the cold weather and the forecasted early snowstorm. Now — corny as it sounded — the weather didn't matter. You'd think he'd fallen in love.

David grabbed the ends of the bath towel dangling against his bare chest and scrubbed them over his still-damp hair as he walked back to the bathroom. That's exactly what had happened. He'd fallen in love with the Lord. He shook his head, tossed the towel over the edge of the tub and squirted toothpaste on his toothbrush. David Carlson — a born-again Christian! *Unbelievable!*

David scrubbed his teeth, shaved off his five-o'clock shadow, splashed on some citrus cologne and crossed to his dresser. His face smiled back at him from the mirror as he pulled on a T-shirt and his favorite blue sweater. He stuffed his wallet into the back pocket of his jeans, then lifted the small velvet-covered ring box sitting on top of the dresser into his hand.

The thing he couldn't get over was how *light* he felt. It was the strangest thing. He felt as if a burden had been lifted from him, and he hadn't even been aware he was carrying one around. He couldn't wait to tell Erin about his experience of accepting Jesus as his Lord!

David grabbed his jacket, stuck the ring box in one pocket, his cell phone in the other and whistled his way down the short hall to the entrance. *Erin, here I come — a new man in the Lord! Nothing will stand in our way now.* He grabbed his keys, flipped off the lights and trotted out the door and down the stairs.

The lock bar was cold to his touch. David shoved open the safety door to the garage, shivering as a blast of cold air hit him. Maybe it *would* snow! Good! The park would be empty for sure. An image of himself proposing to Erin while snow swirled around the gazebo flashed into his mind.

David grinned, tightened his fingers around his car keys and shoved his hands into his pockets for warmth as he loped toward his car.

The shot took him in the left shoulder.

"Ugh!" David's hands tightened in reflex on the items in his pockets. Shock rippled through him as the impact of the bullet toppled him backward. He yanked a hand free to catch himself, but it was too late. There was a bright flash of light as his head slammed against the concrete floor. And then there was nothing.

Erin stepped through the door into the kitchen, kicked it closed behind her and shoved the bags in her arms onto the counter. Tonight was her night. She was going to relax and get a good night's sleep if it killed her! She was tired of dry, burning eyes with lilac-colored bags beneath them and a mind that felt as if it were stuffed with cotton batting.

She flipped on the lights, turned the oven to warm and placed the chicken portobello she'd picked up on her way home inside. The slice of strawberry cheesecake, she put in the refrigerator alongside the chocolate wafers she intended to eat while soaking in a relaxing aromatherapy bath.

Erin lifted the bag with the herbal bath mix, the various-sized candles, the matching scented soap and shampoo and the new luxurious bath towel into her arms and started for the stairs. She wanted everything ready, so she could just go from dinner, to bath, to bed without having to stop and prepare.

She hummed softly as she closed the tub drain, spilled in the contents of the herbal bath package, set out the soap and shampoo then arranged the candles on the wide ledge at the end of the tub. The remaining candles she clustered on the sink. A book of matches went beside them.

"Umm." She rubbed the luxurious softness of the thick new towel against her cheek, then hung it over the bar and went into the bedroom to turn down her bed and bring back her coziest pair of pajamas. There! She gave a satisfied glance at her book and CD player waiting within arm's reach on the hamper — the volume on the player already turned down low — and smiled. Everything was ready.

Now for dinner.

Erin trotted down to the kitchen to turn off the oven. She pulled a crocheted table mat and flatware from a drawer and carried them to a TV tray in the living room. No more silent meals of cold, tasteless sandwiches. Tonight she was feasting in style. She'd have an old sitcom for company, one that would make her laugh. She picked up the remote, clicked on the TV and headed for the kitchen to get her meal.

". . . repeat, David Carlson, award-winning reporter for *The Herald* —"

"No!" Erin whirled about and ran for the control to switch channels.

". . . was shot this evening in the parking garage of his apartment complex —"

Her heart stopped. Her lungs quit. She couldn't move, couldn't hear. She stood frozen, staring in horror at the woman mouthing words on the TV screen. *Lord Jesus, help me hear! I have to know! David! Oh, dear Lord, not David.*

". . . by ambulance to Goodhope Memorial Hospital. We've learned through reliable sources that Mr. Carlson's condition is critical. Police are . . ."

Her legs flexed. Her hands twitched. The movement broke the emotional paralysis, brought her to herself. Erin spun about and ran to the kitchen, snatching her car keys off the counter and slamming through the door into the garage. *Thirty minutes to Goodhope Hospital. Thirty minutes to reach David! Thirty minutes — an eternity.*

She started the car, backed out and headed toward downtown. The snow hurled itself against the windshield, and she automatically turned on the wipers. Clutching the wheel in a death grip, she willed other vehicles out of her path. "Let him live, Lord! Don't let him die. Oh, God, please don't let David die!"

An ambulance pulled in behind her, lights flashing a message of urgency as it stopped in front of the emergency room entrance. Erin parked, jerked from her car, slammed the door and ran around the large vehicle to the electric glass doors. They slid open with an ominous whisper. She dashed through, glanced around then rushed to the admittance desk. "David Carlson, p-please." She clamped her jaws together to stop her teeth from chattering.

The receptionist tapped some keys, then glanced up from her computer. "He's been taken to surgery. The waiting room is on the third floor — west wing. Use the elevators at the end of the hall."

Surgery! Erin fought back a surge of panic and sprinted for the elevators, catching one just as the doors started to close. She slid through, glancing at the older woman standing in front of the control panel. "Third floor, please." *Hurry! Hurry!* She wrapped her arms about herself to try to stop the trembling, leaned against the elevator wall and closed her eyes. *Let him live, Lord. Please don't let David be lost. Guide the surgeon's thoughts and hands —*

"Are you all right, dear? You're terribly pale."

Erin opened her eyes. The woman was staring at her, a concerned look on her face. She tried to smile reassurance, but her facial muscles didn't want to work. She nodded, then jolted erect as the elevator stopped. The doors slid open. She darted out into the hall, scanned the wall for signs directing the way then rushed to the waiting room.

A gray-haired woman sitting at a table facing the door smiled at her as she stopped and looked around to get her bearings. "May I help you?"

"Yes, thank you. It's —" Erin took a breath, made a valiant effort to stop shivering and chattering as she moved toward the table. "I was told to wait here."

"You have someone in surgery?"

She nodded. "David Carlson."

The woman lifted the glasses dangling on a chain about her neck to her eyes and looked down at a paper with a list of names on it. "I don't see him listed." A frown creased her forehead. "Who is his doctor?"

Erin stared at the woman, fighting back another surge of panic. "I don't know. He was . . . shot. They brought him here. I heard it on the TV." She shuddered and rubbed her hands up and down her arms trying to create some warmth.

"Oh, my dear, how horrible for you!" The glasses fell back to rest against the woman's ample bosom, the fine chain catching on a name tag that read Mrs. Harrison. "His name won't be on the list if he wasn't scheduled. I'll have to call down for information." She reached for the phone. "Are you a member of Mr. Carlson's family?"

Erin shook her head. "David doesn't have any family here. He's my —" Panic grabbed her again. *How could she explain their relationship so they'd give her information?* She took a breath. "My not-quite fiancé."

"I see. And your name is?"

"Erin Kelly."

"Very well, Miss Kelly, you may have a seat while I phone down to surgery and see what I can find out for you." The woman gestured toward the padded chairs and settees arranged around small tables covered with lamps and magazines. "I'll come tell you as soon as I have any information."

"Thank you." Erin nodded and walked to the closest chair, closing her eyes as she yielded herself to its welcome support. *Lord, please let the news be good. Please let David be all right. Please don't let him —*

"Coffee?"

Erin popped her eyes open. A thin, stylishly dressed middle-aged woman smiled and held a foam cup out to her. "There's a machine in the corner. It's not the best coffee I've ever tasted, but it's hot, and you look like you could use a good hot drink. Cream?" The woman's other, well-manicured hand held two small containers of dairy substitute.

Erin's stomach heaved at the coffee aroma. She forced her lips to curve upward. "You're very kind." She reached for the cup, but her hands were shaking so hard she was afraid to take it.

"Why don't I just put it here?" The woman placed the cup on the table beside Erin's chair. "I heard what you said. You must have been very frightened to leave home without a coat in this weather."

"What?"

The woman pointed.

Erin glanced down. Small clumps of snow were melting into her sweater. She brushed them away.

"I pray your young man will be all right."

Her throat tightened. "Thank you."

The woman smiled and patted her hand. "Mrs. Armstrong?"

Erin glanced beyond the woman. A doctor in surgical scrubs stood just inside the door scanning a questioning gaze over the people in the room.

"Here I am, Doctor." The woman drew in a deep breath and turned around. Two young people rose from their chairs and joined her as she and the doctor walked toward a small private nook off to one side of the room.

Erin pushed the coffee farther away and closed her eyes. *She's frightened, Lord. Please let her loved one be all right. And please save David, he —*

"Miss Kelly."

She looked up at Mrs. Harrison.

The woman smiled. "They're almost finished in surgery. I told them you were here. The surgeon, Dr. Walters, will come talk with you shortly." She hurried back to her desk to answer the ringing phone.

Erin gripped the arms of the chair to keep from rising and chasing after the woman. She'd told her *nothing!* Where had the bullet struck David? What was the operation? Why was he critical?

Critical! The fear coiled and struck again. It was all Erin could do to sit still. She wanted to moan and wail and rock to and fro to ease the solid knot of terror twisting her insides. She wrapped her arms about herself and closed her eyes again, shutting out the sights and sounds of the room as she prayed.

"Erin Kelly?"

Erin opened her eyes. There was another doctor dressed in blue scrubs standing at the door, searching the waiting room with his gaze. Gray hair peaked out from under his cloth cap, a mask hung loose under his chin. Dread pounced. She wanted to run and hide. Instead she rose to her feet — swayed forward. "I'm Erin Kelly."

The doctor glanced her way, hurried over and took hold of her arm. "Why don't we sit right here while we talk, Miss Kelly?" He eased her back down into the chair, his fingers slipping to the inside of her wrist. "Mr. Carlson came through the surgery fine. The bullet passed through his shoulder without hitting any bone. . . ."

His shoulder! Not his heart or lungs or — Relief flooded her. Erin yanked her thoughts back to the doctor.

". . . a matter of removing foreign material and closing." His gaze scanned her face. He gave a tiny nod and lifted his hand from her wrist. "There is a tube in place for drainage of the wound, but that is normal procedure and will be removed as healing progresses. Do you have any questions?"

She forced out words. "He's no longer . . . critical?"

The doctor rubbed his hand over the back of his neck and gave her a kind look. "I'm a surgeon, Miss Kelly, not a diagnostician. You'll have to talk to the admitting doctor about Mr. Carlson's medical condition. All I can tell you is that the surgery went well." He rose. "Now, if you'll excuse me, I have to get back to work. Barring any complications, Mr. Carlson should be out of recovery and in his bed in ICU within the hour."

ICU. Erin's relief dissolved. She took a breath. "Thank you, Doctor."

He nodded and hurried away.

Erin rose and walked from the small chapel to the elevator, stepping inside and pushing the button for the fourth floor. Never had an hour seemed so long. Usually, when she prayed the time sped by, but now she was aware of every minute — every second. Of course, she'd prayed with part of her listening for the phone. The doctor had promised they'd call her in the chapel if anything —

Erin jerked her thoughts from the dire possibilities. She needed to concentrate on the positive. "In everything give thanks: for this is the will of God in Christ Jesus concerning you." She quoted the scripture verse and closed her eyes. "Thank You, Lord, that they didn't have to call me. Thank You, that —"

The elevator stopped, the doors slid open. Erin stepped out into the ICU waiting area, skimming her gaze over an older couple sitting on a settee holding hands and staring at the floor, a middle-aged man standing by the window drinking coffee and a young couple selecting crackers and juice from an array on a wheeled cart. The tense atmosphere of the place brought her shivers back full force.

The man at the window looked her way and gave a small, polite nod of greeting. "You're new. You have to let them know you're here and tell them who you want to see." He gestured toward the closed double doors leading to the unit. "There's an intercom over there."

"Thank you." Erin hurried toward the doors and her heart sank. A sign over the intercom read Immediate Family Only. *Please, Lord, intervene. Make them let me in.* She keyed the intercom.

"Yes?"

"Erin Kelly to see David Carlson please."

"A moment."

Please, Lord!

A buzzer sounded. Erin pushed through the doors. A dark-haired nurse smiled at her. "He's in the first bed on your right."

Erin nodded her thanks, pivoted on her heel and stepped through the curtained opening into the small cubicle, her heart jolting violently at the sight that greeted her. All she could see of David was his head. His face was still and pale. Various tubes flowed under the blankets that covered him and machines whirred and ticked in the background. But it didn't matter. Nothing mattered but that he was alive.

The sights, sounds and smells combined with the relief of seeing David made her light-headed. Erin grabbed for the end of his bed to steady herself and inched forward along the side until she was close to his chest. "David?"

He didn't respond. Panic edged into her. The admitting doctor's words wriggled like snakes through her mind. *Severe blow to the back of his head . . . concussion . . . swelling of brain tissue . . . loss of consciousness . . . no bleeding.*

Erin grabbed onto the sliver of hope. *Thank You, Lord, he isn't bleeding.* She leaned closer and raised her voice to a normal level. "David?"

"He's not answering anyone just yet."

Erin twisted around toward the door. The dark-haired nurse smiled and walked to the head of the bed, checking the IVs and monitors. "You're just having yourself a nice rest, aren't you, Mr. Carlson?" She lifted the blanket.

Erin gasped. A bulky bandage traveled over David's wounded shoulder, across his bare chest and under his right arm.

"Impressive, isn't it?"

There was a smile in the nurse's voice. Erin glanced at her.

"It's not as bad as it looks. The wound is here." The nurse indicated a spot where the bandage looked thickest. "The rest is only to hold the drain in place and immobilize his arm and shoulder. We don't want him moving it around and hurting himself when he wakes up." She took hold of David's hand and leaned over, watching him closely. "It's Jean, your annoying nurse, Mr. Carlson. If you can hear me, blink your eyes for me."

Please, Lord! Tears clogged Erin's throat — there wasn't even a tiny flicker of David's eyelids.

"How about my hand, Mr. Carlson — can you squeeze my hand?"

Erin cleared the lump from her throat.

235

"May I hold his hand?"

The nurse nodded. "Of course. Dr. Walters noted on his chart you're Mr. Carlson's fiancée. If anyone can make him want to come back and join us it will be you." She smiled. "Love's a very powerful force, Miss Kelly, so please, touch him. Talk to him. Let him know you're here with him." She checked David's pupils, then reached for his wrist, her eyes fastened on her watch.

Erin lifted the blanket on her side, took hold of David's free hand and leaned over him. "David, it's Erin. I'm here, David. Do you hear me? Do you know I'm with you?" Tears fell from her eyes onto his face. She wiped them away, fighting for control. "David, please blink your eyes or squeeze my hand to let me know you hear me." She lifted his limp hand in both of hers and pressed her damp cheek against it. "Squeeze my hand, David. You can do it — I know you can." Her voice broke on a sob. "Oh, David, *please* hear me! Please blink your eyes, David."

She didn't cry again. She shivered and shook. Her teeth clattered together, but she didn't cry. Her tears were dammed up behind a wall of fear. Erin pounded and battered at the wall with her prayers, but it

236

stood firm. No matter how she fought it, the knowledge that David could die — or live in this comatose state — clung like a burr to her consciousness. And every time she thought about it, the wall of fear grew higher.

"How's he doing? Any response?"

Erin jolted and looked over her shoulder at the nurse coming in the door. "Nothing, yet." She glanced up at the clock — fifteen minutes exactly since the last visit.

The nurse nodded. "It's early, yet." She went about her routine of checking the IV drips and monitors. When she moved to the bed to check David's vital signs, Erin let go of his hand and stepped into the restroom.

Thank You for the capable nurse, Lord. And for the advances in medical care. For the doctors and machines. Erin rehearsed her litany of thanks as she splashed cold water on her face and patted it dry. It helped. She didn't feel quite so giddy and disconnected. She threw the towel in the trash and hurried back to David. The nurse was taking his pulse.

She walked to the bed and took hold of his other hand. "I'm back, David. It's Erin. Can you hear me?" Nothing. *Lord, please* —

"Mr. Carlson, it's your nurse, Jean. If you

237

can hear me, blink your eyes." The nurse's fingers were on his pulse, and she was watching a monitor. "Speak to him again, Miss Kelly."

Erin darted a glance at her, then leaned over the bed. "David, it's Erin." The nurse motioned her to continue. Erin's heart thudded. "David, can you hear me? Do you know I'm here with you?" Her voice broke. "Please answer me, David."

The nurse nodded and released David's wrist. "Keep talking to him, Miss Kelly. If you run out of things to say, tell him about a book you've read or a movie you've seen. But keep talking." She left the cubicle.

Erin stared after the nurse. She wanted to ask, in the worst way, why she wanted her to keep talking to David, but she was too frightened to inquire. If it was something gone wrong, she didn't want to know. She was having enough trouble keeping her faith intact. She looked back down at David. Maybe it was something good. Maybe the nurse thought he could hear even if he didn't respond.

Erin snagged onto the slim thread of hope and squared her shoulders. If David could hear, he mustn't know she was afraid. She cleared her throat and willed her voice to come out sounding normal. "David, something wonderful has happened." She stroked his flacid fingers, swallowing hard at the memory of how strong his hand had felt holding hers. "Janet Wallace's ex-foreman read your article about her difficulty finding employment because she's unable to fill out applications. The company called her back to work, David! And the plant will now give oral tests for job promotions to anyone who can not read or write as long as they come to the center to learn! Do you hear me, David?" Erin blinked tears from her eyes and watched his face for any sign of response. "She has her job back, and many more have a chance at promotions, because of the story *you* wrote! You're a wonderful, talented writer, David. Your words touch people's hearts."

There was no response. Erin looked down at his limp hand and sobs pushed into her throat. Would David ever write again? Her knees buckled. She sank onto the plastic chair and leaned forward to press her cheek against their joined hands, fighting back the fear. *Lord, please — please make David well. Please help him to be able to write again.*

"Miss Kelly, your mother was here. She left you a message." The new night nurse handed her a folded slip of paper, then began her check on David.

Erin's heart pounded. *Her mother knew!* She stepped back out of the way and opened the note, devouring the words.

Erin,
I heard about David on the TV, and I knew you would rush here to be with him. I want you to know your father and I are praying for you both — and that I've put David on the prayer list for area churches. You are not standing alone, Erin. Be strong. Remember, our God hears the cries of His children. I know everything is going to be all right. We love you, honey.

Mom and Dad

The burden of fear weighing her down lightened. Erin took a deep breath and wiped the damp off her cheeks. Her mom and dad were praying for David — and her mom said everything would be all right. She glanced over at David lying immobile in the bed and took another breath. In the face of things it was silly, but her mom's words still made it better.

"Visiting hours are now over. Good evening, everyone."

The quiet announcement coming over the

speakers brought a surge of anxiety, disrupting the momentary easing of her nerves. Erin stepped to the bed and took hold of David's hand, casting the nurse an imploring look. "Please let me stay. I don't want to leave David. I give you my word I won't even talk. I'll just sit here and hold his hand."

The nurse looked down at her own fingers fastened on David's pulse and smiled. "We want you to talk to him, Miss Kelly. You're good for Mr. Carlson, his heart rate increases slightly when you speak."

Erin's breath caught. "What does that mean? Is he getting better? Does he know I'm here?"

"I believe he does, on some level. So we'll break another rule and let you stay with him tonight."

"Another rule?"

The nurse nodded. "The one about immediate family members only. The record says you're his fiancée —" she pointed across the bed at Erin's and David's joined hands "— you're not wearing a ring, Miss Kelly."

Erin darted a look at her bare left hand, then lifted her gaze to the nurse's face. "I told them —"

The nurse raised her hand. "No corrections, Miss Kelly, please." She smiled. "They're bad for our records. We'll let the doctor's notation stand." Her smile widened. "What we don't *know* is good for Mr. Carlson." She tucked David's arm back under the covers and walked out the door.

Tears welled into Erin's eyes at the nurse's kindness. She lifted his hand to her cheek and leaned over him. "The nurse is going to let me stay, David. I don't have to leave. I *won't* leave you — I promise." She leaned down and kissed him. There was no reaction.

The dam broke. Tears gushed. Erin pressed her face against David's neck and buried her sobs in the blanket covering his good shoulder.

CHAPTER SEVENTEEN

It was the longest night of her life. Every hour the nurse came in to check on David, and the result was always the same. No response. She began to dread the visits — they chipped away at her hope, gnawed holes in her faith.

Erin shifted her position in the hard plastic chair and pulled the blanket the nurse had brought her more closely about her shoulders. She couldn't get warm. Couldn't stop shivering. She felt exhausted, but not sleepy — empty, but not hungry. She glanced at their joined hands. Hers was numb from holding David's, but she refused to let go of him. She was *afraid* to let go of him. She changed hands, quietly enduring the prickly pain of the numb hand coming back to life as she wiggled her fingers. She stretched her free arm, rotated her shoulders then quickly pulled the blanket back over her.

"This might warm you a little."

Erin glanced at the cup of coffee the night nurse — what was her name? Lisa? Yes, Lisa — held out to her. "Thanks. I don't know why I'm so cold." She smiled her appreciation and took the cup in her free hand.

"It's lack of sleep, lack of food and reaction to the shock of what's happened." The nurse shook her head. "We don't like it when people we love are hurt. And we certainly aren't used to them getting shot."

Erin gave a violent shudder at her words and coffee sloshed to the brim of the cup. She put it down before she spilled it.

The nurse walked to the head of the bed and bent over David. "Do you hear that, Mr. Carlson? You've got your girlfriend shivering and shaking over you." She chattered away at David while she checked his vital signs, replaced the bag of liquid on the IV pole and adjusted the flow.

Erin watched in silent admiration. How did nurses stay so cheerful in the face of suffering? *Bless them, Lord, for helping David and the others in their care. Give them wisdom and skill to know what is right to do.*

"There we are, all set till next time." The nurse patted David's good shoulder. "I'll be back, Mr. Carlson. I have one more check on you before the shift changes — and next time I want to see the color of your eyes!" She tossed Erin a smile. "You should go get yourself some breakfast and a few hours of sleep."

Erin nodded and returned her smile. "I will after David wakes up."

The nurse glanced back at David. "He's a good-looking one, but there isn't any man handsome enough to make me miss my breakfast, as you can probably tell." She laughed and patted her ample hips as she hurried out of the room.

I want to see them, too, Lord. Please heal David. Please let me see his blue eyes again. Another shiver chased down her spine, spreading throughout her body. Erin reached for the coffee.

Don't be a coffee snob, David.

The words she'd spoken at their impromptu picnic in the park flashed into her mind. She stared down at the cup, her heart knocking against her ribs. She'd read somewhere that the sense of smell was powerful in bringing back memories, and David *loved* coffee.

Erin's pulse pounded. She ran into the bathroom for a small paper cup and poured a little of the hot, strong smelling brew in it. *Please, Lord, wake David up!* She leaned over him, waving the coffee under his nose and forced a cheerful note into her voice. "David, it's Erin. Want to share my morning coffee?" She held the cup closer to his nose. "David, want some coffee?"

"Not with all that cream you put in it."

"David!" The cup dropped from her hand, splashing coffee onto the blanket. Erin stared down into David's eyes — his beautiful blue eyes — for the instant before his eyelids slid closed again.

"David? Nurse!" Erin whipped around and ran for the doorway. *"Nurse!"*

Lisa came running. "What is it?" She brushed past Erin and hurried to the bed, her gaze scanning the monitors.

"He woke up!" Erin's legs gave out. She sagged against the pole holding the curtain, then slid down it and collapsed into a heap on the floor, laughing and crying, shivering and shaking. "David woke up. He smelled the coffee and he woke up!"

"We've finished changing Mr. Carlson's dressing, and you can come back in now, Miss Kelly." The buzzer sounded.

Erin pushed open the door, stepped back into the unit and hurried to David's cubicle. Lisa was raising the head of his newly changed bed.

"Feel better?"

Heat climbed into Erin's cheeks. She smiled and lifted her orange juice container in a salute to the nurse. "Yes, I'm still a little woozy, but you were right, the juice and crackers helped. I'm sorry I made a fuss. I —" She looked at David and tears welled into her eyes. "It was just such a shock! He looked right at me and said he didn't want the coffee with cream in it!"

The nurse laughed. "Not the usual comment a patient makes when they first wake up."

Erin smiled. "David's not your usual guy." She put her juice on the roll-around bed table and studied his face. "He looks different."

"That's because he's sleeping naturally."

"Really?" She folded back the clean blanket and took hold of David's hand. His fingers twitched, then closed around hers for a moment. Joy gushed through her. "He moved!"

"Yes, he's becoming more and more responsive."

"Lisa, you're needed at bed five."

The nurse glanced at the intercom. "On my way." She smiled at Erin and headed for the door. "I'll be back."

"Okay." Erin tucked a strand of hair that had fallen out of the restraining elastic band at the crown of her head behind her ear and looked down — straight into David's open eyes. "Oh!" Her heart slammed against her ribs. His hand tightened on hers.

"Hello, gorgeous."

She couldn't talk. Couldn't think. She just stared at David, drinking in the sight of him awake, aware, *alive.* His gaze shifted, came back. A frown creased his forehead.

"Where am I?"

His raspy voice broke her momentary mental block. She pushed an answer out of her constrictive throat. "You're in the hospital."

Shock swept over his face. "Why? Did I have an accident?"

Erin shook her head. "No, you were shot." Her lips trembled. "David, you were *shot!*" She wilted against the bed, her free hand sliding up and brushing against the rough stubble on his jaw as she buried her face in the crook of his neck and sobbed her relief out on his good shoulder.

Erin splashed water on her face and dabbed herself with a paper towel. She loosened her hair to comb it with her fingers, then caught it back in a bun at the crown of her head with an elasticized fabric band. Wisps fell free around her face and down the back of her neck, but it was the best she could do.

She glanced into the mirror and cringed. She looked horrible. Lavender circles under dark-green eyes did not go well with chili-powder hair. The oatmeal color of the sweater didn't do much for her pale face either.

"Well, what did you expect after thirty-plus hours without sleep?" Erin stuck her tongue out at her reflection, brushed some lint off her jeans and walked back into David's room. She sat in the plastic chair and took hold of his hand, weariness washing over her.

David was still sleeping after his examination by the doctor. She studied him as he slept, her heart filling with thanksgiving at the doctor's prognosis for his full recovery, but beneath the deluge of joy ran an undercurrent of sorrow. She would have to give him up all over again.

Erin turned her thoughts from that truth. She wasn't ready to acknowledge it — couldn't bear the pain of it on top of all that had happened. Until he was pronounced well — until David was able to go home — she would stay with him and cherish the gift of time spent together.

"Miss Kelly . . . elly . . . elly."

Erin jolted erect and shook her head to clear it of the echoing voice. She forced her eyes open. David's nurse was standing beside her chair.

"It's time for you to go home, Miss Kelly."

"But —"

The nurse shook her head. "No buts. Mr. Carlson has passed the crisis. He's scheduled for a few tests this afternoon, and if all goes as expected, he'll be transferred to a regular room where he'll sleep the rest of the night. He needs the rest, and so do you. Go home and come back to see him tomorrow morning."

Erin struggled to process the nurse's words. Her head felt thick and heavy and she couldn't quite grasp her thoughts.

The nurse gave her an understanding smile. "You won't be allowed to stay with Mr. Carlson, tonight, Miss Kelly. When there's no crisis, the rules apply."

"The rules — I understand." Erin rose from the chair, her legs wobbling beneath her. She grabbed the edge of the bed and leaned over David. "I have to go, David, but I'll be back in the morning." She kissed him, delighted when his lips made a slight response.

"Call someone to come after you, Miss Kelly. You're too tired to drive."

Erin smiled as the nurse's voice re-bounded through her head. She walked out of the cubicle and through the double doors, then punched the down button on the elevator.

David! She'd let go of him! Erin groped for David's hand — something jingled — something hard and cold. There was nothing else but the softness of a blanket beneath her fingers. She started awake, staring in confusion at the coverlet under her. Her coverlet. She pushed herself to a sitting position and swept her gaze around her bedroom. How did she get home? The cars keys gripped in her hand gave her the answer.

She dropped the keys and scooted over to the side of the bed. Erin rubbed her finger-tips over her eyelids, temples and forehead, trying to brush away the cobwebs clouding her mind. Try as she might, the last thing she could remember was getting in the el-evator.

Erin gave her head a quick shake, opened her eyes and glanced at her alarm clock. Seven o'clock! She had slept around the clock and then some. She had to call the hospital! She rose to her feet, slipped on her shoes and hurried downstairs for the phone book to look up the number.

David was doing fine. He was in room 214. Erin turned the corner, reading the numbers beside the doors ahead of her . . . 206. Her heart thudded, her pulse raced . . . 208. Her mouth was dry, her palms moist and her stomach fluttering like moths around a light. All because she was going to see David. How was she ever going to give him up again? Room 210 . . . 212 . . . 214.

Erin stopped and took a deep breath for control. She had to keep things friendly — only friendly. It wouldn't be fair to either of them to let hope for a deeper relationship with each other blossom again. Of course, David could even have a new interest by now.

The thought made her heart feel like it was bleeding. She took another breath, stepped into the room and stopped — shocked to immobility. David was clean shaven, dressed in surgical scrubs and sitting up in bed talking to a man standing with his back toward the door. The look that sprang into his eyes when he spotted her took her breath away.

"Ah!" The man turned, his friendly face wreathed in a broad smile. "From the look on David's face, you have to be Erin. And I . . . must be leaving." He glanced back over his shoulder as he moved toward the door. "I'll see you tomorrow, David." He glanced at her and smiled. "Hello and good-bye, Miss Kelly." He disappeared into the hallway.

"Hi."

How could such a simple little word make your knees go weak? Erin braced herself against the urge to run to David and pushed a light, friendly tone into her voice. "Hi, yourself." She gestured toward the door. "Who is that?"

"Don Hughs — Pastor Don Hughs."

She grasped the impersonal subject like a lifeline. "Is he the hospital chaplain?"

"Not exactly." David patted the bed beside him. "Come sit down. I've been waiting for you."

"You have?" Erin shrugged off her coat, hung it over the back of a chair and strolled to the bed on his left side. The side with the arm held immobile by the bandage wound around his chest and the hospital shirt that covered it. She felt safer that way. She didn't trust her hand not to betray her by reaching for his. To be sure, she stuck her hands in her blazer's pockets. "And how did you know I'd come?"

David's warm gaze captured hers. "I remember yesterday." His deep voice touched her like a caress. "It was you that pulled me through, Erin. I never wanted anything in my life as much as I wanted to come back to you. Every time you spoke to me, I fought harder."

"David, don't — I can't —" Tears welled into Erin's eyes — overflowed. She lifted her hands to wipe them away.

Before she knew what he was about, David slid his legs over the side of the bed and stood, pulling her against him, holding her close with his free arm. It felt like coming home. She fought the temptation to lean against him, the longing to stay in his arms forever. "Don't cry, Erin. It's all right. I love you, Erin."

"No! We can't! *I* can't." She tried to break free but he held her tight and she was afraid to struggle for fear she might hurt him or pull the IV needle out. She made her body go stiff and unresponsive. "Let me go, David."

"Not yet. I've got something to tell you first. Look at me, Erin."

She steeled herself and lifted her head to meet his gaze.

"I'm born again, Erin."

She stared at him, stupefied by the out-of-left field comment. "What did you say?"

"I said, I'm born again." Joy lit David's face. He smiled and drew her closer. "I accepted Jesus as my Lord and Savior last Wednesday night. I was on my way to tell you when I was shot on Thursday."

"But — I thought you didn't —" The words stuck in her throat, she couldn't say them.

David nodded, his arm tightened. "I thought so, too. But you totally destroyed my life." He smiled and lifted his hand to touch her cheek. Erin's breath caught. "There was something so special about you — so pure and clean — it ruined me for my old way of life. I tried to go back when we said goodbye, but I couldn't."

He threaded his fingers through her hair, cupped the back of her head in his palm. "So I decided to find out what made you so different. I asked Pastor Hughs what you meant when you said that being a Christian isn't only what you believe, it's who you are. And when he explained that Christianity isn't a religion, it's a personal relationship with Jesus and a way of life — I knew I wanted that, too." He looked full into her eyes. "It was what I'd been searching for all along. I just didn't know it until God brought you into my life. And then I was too stubborn and angry about the past to admit it. But that's over now. I'm a born-again Christian."

"Oh, David, I'm so glad! I've prayed so hard!"

He drew her head closer, lowered his forehead to rest against hers. "I love you, Erin."

"I love you, David." His lips brushed hers, tasted of them, claimed them fully. His kiss was sweeter than anything she'd ever known — even if it was salty with her tears of joy.

CHAPTER EIGHTEEN

"Just wanted to let you know you don't have to worry about Angelo Vida anymore." Don Gallo gestured toward the bandage on David's left shoulder. "His shot at you missed the mark. I didn't miss mine. He won't bother anyone ever again."

David nodded, watching as the homicide detective helped himself to a chocolate-covered caramel from the box of candy Ted and Darlene had brought him. "I don't remember anything about last Thursday night. What happened? Why did you come to my parking garage?"

A grin lifted one corner of Gallo's mouth. "Because you're hopeless at watching out for yourself." He shook his head and popped the piece of candy in his mouth. "I never saw a potential target make so many mistakes. When I had to call off the black-and-whites, I figured I'd check around your place whenever I had the chance." His grin widened. "Lucky for you I had a call to make in your neighborhood that night and drove in to check out your place while I was in the area."

David smiled. "I would have called it luck once, but I'm learning better. It was a blessing of the Lord."

Don Gallo gave him a penetrating look, then nodded his head. "Yeah, I've had a few of those. You need them in my line of work." He selected another piece of candy. One with filberts in it.

"And?"

Gallo shrugged. "And when I drove in, you were on the floor with Angelo standing over you taking aim at your head. I laid on the horn and blinded him with my headlights. When I got out of the car, he started running. I hollered for him to stop — he turned and shot at me. He missed. I didn't. End of story."

David was sure it wasn't quite that simple, but he let it go. "So my life is my own again? I don't have to be concerned about someone trying to keep me from testifying at Benny Vida's trial?"

Gallo licked chocolate off his fingers. "You don't have to worry about testifying period. Benny squawked and hollered for a deal when he learned Angelo wasn't around to protect him anymore. The rest of the family doesn't care if he rots in jail forever and he knows it. He agreed to life without parole. He won't be bothering you or anyone else again, either."

Gallo slanted him a look, then fastened his overcoat. "You can go back to wandering the streets of the city in your haphazard fashion without fear —" he grinned again "— unless you get hit by a car jaywalking."

David stood and stuck out his hand. "Thanks for the straight shooting, Gallo. I owe you."

The detective shrugged. "Yeah." He shook David's hand. "Remember that the next time you write a piece about the department. Be a little complimentary. It won't kill you — and neither will the Vidas." He grabbed another caramel, gestured in a mock salute with it and walked out the door.

David sank down onto the edge of the bed, feeling ill at the thought of how close he'd come to becoming another statistic in a homicide file. He took a deep breath and closed his eyes. "Thank You, Lord, for Your protection. I didn't realize how close I came to not being here. Whatever Your purpose was in saving me, give me 'ears to hear,' Lord, that I might know and obey. And thank You for giving me a second chance with Erin. I'll never hurt her again, Lord. By Your grace, I'll never hurt her again."

The nurse hung the new bag of fluid on the IV pole, adjusted the drip, watched for a moment then smiled at him. "All set till next time, Mr. Carlson."

"Thanks."

"You're welcome." She made a note on her pad and hurried on her way.

David rose from the chair, grabbed the pole and wheeled it over to the window. He was restless without Erin. He didn't like it when she was gone. He should have had Ted pick him up a new sweater and jacket to wear home tomorrow. But the truth was, he liked the idea of Erin shopping for his clothes. It was a little taste of the domesticity to come.

He looked at the overcast sky and smiled. A winter storm was forecast. It was supposed to reach them sometime in the wee hours of the morning and continue for three days. Looked as if his vision of —

"Mr. Carlson?"

"Yes?" David turned, sweeping his gaze over the attractive man and woman standing just inside his door. A smile tugged at his lips at sight of the man's head. He now knew where Erin got that chili-powder hair.

"Mr. and Mrs. Kelly?"

"That would be us." Erin's father grinned and ran his fingers through his hair. "How'd you guess?" His wife smiled. It was Erin's smile.

David smiled back. Erin was a true mix of her mom and dad — except for her gorgeous green eyes. Those were Erin's alone. "The hair's a dead giveaway, sir." He shifted his gaze. "And so is your smile, Mrs. Kelly. They make a beautiful combination in your daughter."

Her gaze warmed. "What a lovely thing to say."

"What'd you expect, hon, the man makes his living stringing words together." Mr. Kelly's grin took any possible negative connotation from his words. He placed his hand on his wife's back and propelled her forward, sticking out his other hand. "I'm Michael, and this is Carol."

David took his hand. "And I'm David. It's a pleasure to meet you both." He gestured toward the chairs beside the window. "Won't you have a seat? I'm afraid the chairs aren't very comfortable, but it's all that's available."

Erin's father unzipped his jacket, then reached over to help his wife off with her coat. "I figure they do that on purpose, so people won't stay too long."

"Michael." Erin's mom shot her husband a look.

David laughed, shoved his IV pole back out of the way and sat on the edge of bed. "I think you may be right. I know I feel that way about this bed. I can't leave it soon enough." He forgot and started to use his left hand to boost himself farther back toward his pillows on the raised head. Pain zinged through his wounded shoulder. He winced.

Erin's mother was beside the bed instantly. "Let me help." She grabbed his pillows, fluffed them and stuffed them in behind his back. "There — all set. You can lean back now." She smiled at him, then turned toward the chair with her coat draped over it and sat down.

David settled into a comfortable position, grateful for the moment to gather himself together. It had been twenty-four years since he'd had anyone "mother" him. It filled his heart with an odd sort of longing.

"Are you in much pain, David?"

He shook his head. "Not unless I do something foolish, the way I did a moment ago. Of course, the drugs help." Erin's mom had a beautiful, soft voice. He could almost hear her reading stories and singing lullabies to her children — or grandchildren. That thought curled his lips into a warm smile.

She blinked. "Gracious!" Carol Kelly's own beautiful smile returned. "I can see why Erin was so taken with you, David. That smile would melt any woman's heart." She gave a soft laugh.

David wiggled in discomfort at the compliment and rearranged his features. She crinkled her nose at him — another endearing Erin trait.

"Speaking of Erin, where is she? She said she'd be here."

David shifted his gaze to Erin's father. "There's a possibility the doctor will release me tomorrow morning, so Erin went to buy me a new sweater and jacket to go home in." He tossed them a wry grin. "Between the bullet and the scissors in the E.R. nurse's hand, mine were reduced to rags. She should be back soon."

Michael turned to his wife. "You might as well give it to him while we're waiting for Erin."

She nodded and they both stepped to the bed. Carol smiled and handed him a blue-and-green plaid gift bag.

David reached inside. "Thank you, but you —" He stopped, staring at the black leather study Bible with his name embossed in gold letters on the front.

"Erin told us you've been born again, David." Carol's eyes shimmered with moisture. "Welcome to God's family." She leaned over and kissed him on the cheek.

"Hey! That's *my* man you're kissing, Mom!"

Carol laughed and turned to face her grinning daughter. "Well, turnabout is fair play, young lady! You've been kissing my man all your life."

Erin laughed and hurried to her father. "And I intend to continue." She went on tiptoe and planted a loud smack on her father's cheek. "Hi, Dad."

"Hi, Boots." He returned her hug as best he could with the large parcel she held under one arm.

David raised an eyebrow. "Boots?"

Erin laughed and lifted the package slightly his way. "If you want these clothes, don't ask." She extricated herself from her father's arms and hugged her mother.

It made David feel part of the family just watching them. He reached out and snagged Erin's coat, tugging her to him when she finished hugging her mother. He gave her a light kiss. "Sorry, gorgeous, but I think I have to know about this 'Boots' thing."

"David . . ."

"When Erin was little, she went through a cowgirl phase —"

"Daaaad!"

Erin's father grinned at her and went right on talking over his wife's soft laughter. "For about six months she refused to go anywhere without wearing her cowboy bib and tucker — even to church." He chuckled. "She made quite a picture walking down the aisle in her Sunday best dress, wearing a cowboy hat and boots. Hence the name."

David laughed. "That I'd like to see. I hope you have pictures."

"Oh, indeed we do."

"Mom!" Erin laughed and shook her head. "I give up. I'm surrounded by traitors. And you're the worst of all." She looked down at him, her eyes glowing with love. "I *told* you not to ask."

David's heart thudded. He wanted in the worst way to pull her close and kiss those smiling lips of hers, but not with her parents for an audience. He forced a grin. "I know, but I couldn't resist. Forgive me?"

She crinkled her nose at him. "I forgive you." She tugged her gaze away from his. "Now let's see if this sweater is large enough to slip down over your bandaged shoulder and arm."

David blew out a gust of relief as Erin

reached down to undo the package she'd laid on the bed. If she hadn't broken that look and turned away, he'd have kissed her, parents or no parents. His self-control had a limit — and her name was Erin. He was head over heels in love with her.

CHAPTER NINETEEN

Erin pulled on her black wool pants and green turtleneck sweater, and went back to the bathroom to finish getting ready.

The mirror was still steamed over from her shower. She turned on her blow-dryer and blew the mirror clear, smiling as her reflection appeared. Her eyes were glowing and there was a big smile on her face. In a few minutes she was going to the hospital to take David home.

"Thank You, Jesus!"

Her shout echoed off the glass. Erin laughed and leaned closer to her image. "You are seriously in love, lady." Her eyes twinkled back at her. She winked and turned the blow-dryer on her hair, lifting and fluffing it with her free hand to hasten the drying time of her thick tresses. When she finished, she brushed it until it shone and let it hang loose to sweep against her shoulders. A touch of blusher, some lip balm and she was ready.

Erin hummed her way into the bedroom and laced on her boots. She shrugged into her black wool peacoat then hurried down the stairs, snatching her car keys off the coffee table on her way through the living room.

It was starting to snow as she backed out of the garage.

David paced the room, stopped and shoved his right hand into his jeans pocket again, his fingers searching for the small gold circle. It was still there. Like it could have gone anywhere in the last thirty seconds! He shook his head at his own foolishness and walked to the window to look outside.

It was starting to snow. Excitement tightened his stomach. It wasn't the big fluffy snowflakes falling in the swirling thickness he'd envisioned in his mind, but it was close enough. If only he had two good arms. He wanted to crush Erin to himself, hold her tight and know they'd never be apart again. More foolishness, of course, but it was the way he felt. He just wanted to know she would be his forever! "Lord, please help me not to bungle this!"

Man, he was nervous! David shook his head and walked to the bedside table, crammed the items in the drawer into the plastic bag the hospital had given him and tossed them in the wastebasket. The only things he was taking home from here was the Bible the Kellys had given him and a new beginning.

"Hi, handsome. Going my way?"

David turned. Erin stood in the doorway, her hair falling in a glorious shimmer around her smiling face. The sight of her stole his breath. "Always."

Erin's eyes went soft with love. David sucked in a breath to replace the air the sight of her had knocked out of him and grabbed his jacket. She rushed forward to help him. He jabbed his arm through the right sleeve, clenching his teeth together to keep from reaching for her as she pulled the left side over his useless shoulder. The sleeve dangled empty at his side.

"Do you want your jacket zipped?" Erin looked up and their gazes met.

David figured if he stuck his fingers in an electric socket it would give him less of a jolt than looking into her eyes. *Be patient! Wait!* He shook his head. "No, this is all right. Let's just get out of here." He patted his pocket one more time to be sure everything was secure, then picked up his new Bible and followed her out the door.

■ ■ ■ ■

"Why do you want to go by the park?" Erin reached out and flicked the windshield wipers up to high speed. The snow was starting to come fast and furious.

"There's something I have to do."

"You're going to get out of the car in this weather?" Erin shot him a concerned look, then turned her attention back to the road. "Do you think that's a good idea, David? I don't think you should get chilled." She shot him another look. "What if you catch a cold or something?"

"I'm not worried about getting chilled." *Quite the opposite.* "This jacket is plenty warm."

"Well . . ."

It was obvious she was uneasy about the idea. *Great! What a time to have their first disagreement.* "It won't take long — five minutes maybe." He indicated the turn ahead. "Park close to the gazebo."

Erin flashed him a baffled look and made the turn. There were no other vehicles in the area. She pulled into the parking slot closest to the walk leading to the gazebo and looked at him. "Do you want me to wait here for you, or —"

"No." David almost smiled. For once his useless arm was coming in handy. "I might need your help."

"All right." Erin cut the motor, unlatched her seat belt and reached for the door handle.

"Wait, Erin." She paused. He smiled. "This is one thing I can still handle."

David climbed out of the car, slammed the door and walked around the front of the vehicle. He opened Erin's door and took her hand. The snow was falling so fast and thick around them he could barely see her as she rose to stand beside him. "Come on!" He tugged her hand and started up the path.

The snow falling outside made the gazebo seem small and intimate. David's heart thundered. He'd never in his life felt like this!

Erin glanced around the small empty space, then shot him a quizzical look. "Well, what do you want me to do?"

"Come here." David tightened his grip on her hand and cleared his throat. "Erin, I was attracted to you the moment I saw you. And every time I saw you the attraction grew stronger." He released her hand and lifted his to touch her face, to thread his fingers through her hair and cup her head, drawing her close. "I fell in love with you right here in this park, playing a word game and sheltering ourselves from the rain in this gazebo."

"Oh, David —" Erin's voice was soft with love.

"Shh, Erin. Let me get this out of my heart." He took a deep breath, fighting to control his need to hold her tight. "That was the first time I held you in my arms — and I've never been the same. Every time I have to let you go, my arms feel emptier and my heart feels lonelier. These past few weeks without you were a living death for me."

He let her go, reached into his pocket and withdrew the ring, holding it out to her. "I know of only one solution to the problem. Erin Kelly, will you marry me?"

"Yes!" Erin wrapped her arms about his neck and hugged him fiercely. As she drew back, she wiped away the tears of happiness streaming down her face and held out her left hand. "A thousand times yes, David!"

He looked deep into her eyes, slipped the ring on her finger then encircled her waist with his arm and pulled her close against him, aching with love for her. "I'll love you forever, Erin." His voice was a husky choked whisper.

"Forever, David." Erin sighed and slid her arms back up around his neck as he lowered his lips to hers, sealing their promise with a kiss.

EPILOGUE

"I wish you could be here, Alayne."

"So do I, Boots. But it wouldn't work — I'd only ruin your special day for everyone."

Erin drew her breath to protest.

Her sister gave a bitter laugh. "And don't say I wouldn't. You know as well as I do that I cast a cloud over Mom and Dad's happiness."

"I know, Alayne, but it's only because they love you and —"

"I know why it is, Boots." There was a sudden blast of honking horns in the background. "Look, I've got to go. I'm pulling into Denver and I have to pay attention to traffic. Have a great day, Boots. And give that handsome hunk of a man you're marrying a hug and a kiss for me!" There was a pause. "Give Mom and Dad a kiss for me, too." Another pause. "Be happy, Boots — you deserve it. Love you. Bye."

"Bye, Alayne. I love you."

Erin sat looking down at the cell phone in her hand, then sighed and put it back in her bag. "Lord, help Alayne find true love, and help her find her way back to You. Dear Lord, help her stop running away. I ask it in Your holy name."

She took a deep breath and rose to her feet at a soft tap on the door. "Yes?"

The door opened and her mother stepped into the room. "It's time to start getting ready, Erin. Were you able to get a little rest?"

Erin grinned. "Who can rest with a flock of birds fluttering their wings in your stomach?"

Her mother laughed. "Nervous?"

Erin shook her head. "No — excited." She held out her arms and gave a little twirl. "I can't believe that in two hours and ten minutes I will be Mrs. David Carlson."

"Not if you don't start getting ready, you won't." Her mother blew her a kiss and turned back toward the door. "I'll tell Beverly you're ready for her to do your hair."

"Mom, wait."

Her mother stopped with her hand on the doorknob. "What is it, honey?"

She took a breath. "Alayne called to wish me well. She said to give you and Dad a hug and a kiss for her."

Pain flashed across her mother's face, stealing the happy twinkle from her eyes. It was quickly masked by a smile. "We never should have named that girl Alayne Rae — it means beautiful deer. And you know how swiftly a deer can run." Her voice trembled. "Thank you for telling me, Erin, it helps. Now, I'll just go get Beverly. Time is fleeing!" She hurried out the door.

Erin sighed — even from over two thousand miles away Alayne's rebellion had dampened her mother's pleasure. Well, she wouldn't allow her mom to be sad — not today. Today was about the miracle of a love blessed by the Lord!

She pushed all thought of Alayne out of her mind and began to get ready.

"Erin you look beautiful!" Darlene smiled. "Not that you don't always, but . . . wow!" She laughed. "David's not going to be able to say, 'I do.' He's not going to be able to talk at all when he sees you."

"He'd better say, 'I do.' " Erin laughed and hugged Darlene. "I'm not going through all this tortuous preparation to walk away from the altar empty-handed."

"Erin Kelly!" Her mother put her hand on her chest and feigned shock. "You sound like a huntress."

Erin wiggled her eyebrows and gave a growl low in her throat. "Grrrrrrrrrr! Gonna go get my man!"

"Erin!" Her mother collapsed in helpless laughter. "I don't know where you get your behavior."

Erin flashed her a mischievous look. "From Dad." The long, softly flared skirt of her pure white gown rustled softly as she stepped to the dressing table bench and sat down.

"You look wonderful in that light blue color, Darlene. The dress is gorgeous on you." Erin smiled. "I'll have to make sure and ask you the color of it when David is with me. I want to see his face when you say 'cloud.' "

She glanced at the clock and sobered. "Mom, come put my veil on, please. I can't manage it with all these curls hanging down the back of my head and it's almost time for you to leave. It will take ten minutes to get there."

"Okay, I think that's it. I'm ready." Erin's stomach quivered with nervous excitement. "Something old —" her hand lifted to the crown of her head "— Grandma Kelly's hairpins. Something new —" she looked down "— my gown. Something borrowed

—" she glanced at the bouquet waiting by the door "— Mom's white bride's Bible. And something blue —" Her gaze returned to the bouquet. There were tiny blue flowers and loops of narrow blue lace peeking out here and there among the white roses. "That's everything."

"Not quite. Do you have a penny in your shoe?"

Erin stared at Darlene. "A penny!" She whirled to face her mother. "Mom, where's your purse? I don't have a penny for my shoe!"

"I didn't bring my purse."

She spun around. "Darlene?"

Her matron of honor shook her head. "Sorry, Erin, I left my purse in the car when Ted dropped me off."

Tears sprang to Erin's eyes. "I can't get married without a penny in my shoe!"

Her mother smiled and patted her arm. "Don't worry, honey, Dad will have a penny. You can put it in your shoe when he comes to get you. Now, it's time for Darlene and I to go so we'll be in place when you get there." She slid her arms under the veil and gave her a hug. "I love you, honey." Her voice choked with emotion. "Be happy."

"I will, Mom. I love you, too."

The door closed behind them. Erin

blinked the mist of tears from her eyes and prayed for calm. It was only a penny. It really wasn't important — it was only that she wanted everything to be *perfect* today. Oh, why had she rented this hotel room! She should have dressed at home, even if it did mean a long drive. She would have had a penny at home!

Erin blew out a long gust of air and walked to the mirror to check her appearance one last time. She was being silly. There were far more important things to think about than a penny!

A soft tap on the door yanked her from her thoughts. "Ready, Boots?"

Erin smiled as her father's muffled voice came through the door, calling his pet name for her. She took a deep breath, picked up the Bible and her bouquet, and opened the door. "I'm ready, Dad."

Her father's eyes filled with tears as he gazed down at her. He swallowed hard, leaned down and kissed her cheek. "You're beautiful, honey — just beautiful. David Carlson is one blessed man."

"Thanks, Dad. My, you look so *handsome*." Erin kissed him back, leaned her head against his shoulder for a moment then straightened and looked up at him hopefully. "Do you have a penny, Dad? I need one for my shoe."

A slightly panicked look swept his face. "No I don't, Boots, there's no place in this tux for a wallet. Was I supposed to — nobody told me."

Erin bit down on her lip, trying not to cry, reminding herself it was only a silly tradition. "No, it's my fault, I forgot it. It's okay, Dad. It's not important." She put her hand through his offered arm and walked beside him to the elevator. The doors slid open. And there, laying square in the middle of the elevator floor was a shiny new penny.

Her dad laughed, gently lifted her chin to close her gaping mouth, then knelt down and picked up the penny. "God is interested in even the small things in our lives, Erin. And He always provides." His eyes twinkled up at her as he held out his hand. "Give me your foot, honey, and I'll put God's penny in your shoe."

The day was perfect. The sun spilled golden light and warmth over the earth, creating speckled shadows beneath the leafed-out trees. Flowers bloomed along the paths and in the garden areas of the park. The grass was green and freshly cut, the air redolent with the smell of spring.

Erin caught a glimpse of the gazebo as

her father pulled up and parked in the reserved space. It was outlined with vining flowers and ribbon. Clusters of white wedding bells hanging in the center of each arch swayed softly in a gentle breeze, and a white, flower-bedecked trellis in the center of the gazebo itself formed the altar.

The children from her Sunday school class, all spruced up in their Sunday best and holding baskets full of rose petals to throw in front of her as she walked, lined both sides of the stone path. Friends and family members, fellow workers and students from the center sat on folding chairs facing the gazebo.

Erin caught her breath at the beauty of it all. Her dad opened her door and held out his hand. She rose to stand beside him and heard the music begin.

In the gazebo, the pastor, Darlene and Ted took their places at the altar. David strode forward and descended the steps. Erin's heart swelled with joy at sight of her beloved standing waiting for her. Her eyes filled with tears. "Thank You, Abba Father."

Her dad followed the direction of her gaze and smiled, then offered her his arm.

The music swelled. Step by slow step, Erin walked with her dad along the path, her heart trembling with love. When they reached the steps, her dad placed her hand in David's, kissed her cheek and backed away.

David's hand tightened on hers. She looked up and met his gaze, soft and warm with love for her, and knew she was blessed by the Lord beyond measure. A smile curved her lips. With her hand safe and warm in her beloved's and God's penny in her shoe, she climbed the steps and walked to the altar.

DEAR READER,

One of the most gratifying things about being a writer is having the power to give my characters a happy ending. I do that for all of them — including Erin and David. Unfortunately, it's not always that way in real life. Christians are not perfect, and we sometimes make unwise choices. Like Erin, we close our spiritual ears to that still small voice whispering words of warning and ignore the disquiet in our spirit that tells us there is danger ahead if we continue on the path we have chosen. We put spiritual blinders on and reach for the person or thing that is tempting us, refusing to see any sign that reads Proceed At Peril! And we learn, too late, that what Erin says to her mother is true, "God's laws are not for our restriction — they're for our *protection.*"

I pray the Lord will give you "ears to hear"

and a "heart to obey" — that the paths you walk will all be straight and narrow. And, that if you *do* go astray while reaching for forbidden fruit, you follow Erin's lead, turn quickly and *run* straight back to the forgiving, loving arms of your Heavenly Father. Erin's sister Alayne hasn't learned that lesson — yet. Her story is waiting to be told.

Thank you for choosing *Lessons from the Heart*. I certainly enjoyed writing Erin's and David's story for you. If you care to share your thoughts about the book, I'd like to hear from you. I can be reached at dorothyjclark@hotmail.com.

Until next time,
Dorothy Clark

ABOUT THE AUTHOR

Critically acclaimed, award-winning author **Dorothy Clark** is a creative person. She lives in a home she designed and helped her husband build (she swings a mean hammer!) with the able assistance of their three children. She also designs and helps her husband build furniture. When she is not thus engaged, she can be found cheering her grandchildren on at various sports events, or furiously taking notes about possible settings for future novels as she and her husband travel throughout the United States and Canada. Dorothy believes in God, love, family and happy endings, which explains why she feels so at home writing her stories for Steeple Hill and Steeple Hill Love Inspired. Dorothy enjoys hearing from her readers and may be contacted at dorothyjclark@hotmail.com.

The employees of Thorndike Press hope you have enjoyed this Large Print book. All our Thorndike and Wheeler Large Print titles are designed for easy reading, and all our books are made to last. Other Thorndike Press Large Print books are available at your library, through selected bookstores, or directly from us.

For information about titles, please call:
(800) 223-1244

or visit our Web site at:
www.gale.com/thorndike
www.gale.com/wheeler

To share your comments, please write:
Publisher
Thorndike Press
295 Kennedy Memorial Drive
Waterville, ME 04901

Helw 4.08
AC 8.08

EP NOV 2008

~~CSC~~ JAN 2009
WMV

_ M V MAR 2009
M M E MAY 2009
BMA 1·10
AmcD 8-10
CIR 12·10
MP 2-11
NL 5-11
W M V FEB 2012
MUM 4·12

BE 4-13
mmN 9·13
WMV JUN 2014

Jan 6-21